THE HAWK OF
YONEZAWA

Historical Fiction with J.S. Bach

THE HAWK OF YONEZAWA

Historical Fiction with J.S. Bach

DONALD D. JOYE

ARPress
45 Dan Road Suite 5
Canton MA 02021

Hotline: 1(888) 821-0229
Fax: 1(508) 545-7580

Ordering Information:
Quantity sales. Special discounts are available on quantity purchases by corporations, associations, and others. For details, contact the publisher at the address above.

Printed in the United States of America.

ISBN-13:   Softcover   979-8-89356-868-4
               eBook   979-8-89356-869-1

Library of Congress Control Number: 2024909124

Table of Contents

DEDICATION

A book is always inspired by something. This work is dedicated to two people of great significance in my life: to my oldest son, Colin, whose musicianship and skill at the organ were always a delight and a special gift for his parents, and who performed the identical feat as Bach described herein at a Korean church in Cambridge, Massachusetts, and to Dr. Douglas D. Feaver, scholar, teacher and friend, who introduced me to the personality, life and mission of Johann Sebastian Bach, forever obliterating my previously shallow and superficial understanding of his music, and initiating me into the superbly uplifting, deeply moving, astoundingly beautiful and inspiring music of perhaps its greatest master of all time.

ACKNOWLEDGMENTS

A word of appreciation to those who helped and encouraged me along the tortuous path to publication: to Charles Helmetag, Professor of German and former Chair of Modern Languages at Villanova University, to Patrick Nolan, Professor of English at Villanova, playwright, screenwriter, author of the film *Jericho Mile*, to Terri Valentine, author, critic, line editor and practical teacher, to Mark Spencer, author, critic and teacher. All had a hand in shaping this work from its inception and did their job with patience, encouragement and enjoyment in the work itself. My heartfelt thanks to you all for helping to make this a better read.

As a pronunciation guide, the final "u" in a Japanese word is often not pronounced. Thus, "Hanzu" would be pronounced "Hans," and "gozimasu" would be pronounced "goz-eye-mahss."

CHAPTER 1

THE ROAD BACK

The road to Leipzig stretched out ahead, as it had done for centuries. The stagecoach ambled along at a relaxed pace, kicking up dust occasionally as the wheels hit a soft patch on the road. From the coach, a lone passenger - Johann Sebastian Bach - looked forlornly out the window. He was about fifty-five years old and wore a dark frock coat with knee breeches and buckle shoes. He had a somewhat full head of hair - mostly gray now - combed back all around in the style of the day. He had a foursquare, sturdy form, a little on the heavy side, but not too much. Sturdy really, not fat. He was average height, perhaps a little taller than most. He wore a serious mien with penetrating eyes. His full face had strong features softening a little because of age. On the bench beside him was a Bible, now closed.

The German countryside was beautiful in early fall. Vines would be ripening soon, the juice of their fruit turned into wine by the skillful hand of the vintner. In other locations, rows of hops plants were awaiting their harvest and eventual use in brewing the season's beer. They were cultivated in canopies, the flowers bedecking the supports like garlands surrounding a procession of players at a fête.

Fields of grain grew here and there - wheat and rye mostly, sometimes oats and barley. Copses of trees dotted the landscape frequently - the poplars tall and slender, and the oaks shorter and bushier. The larger woods had pines, lots of evergreen pines. *Tannenbaum* the Germans called them - the symbol of Christmas. Rolling hills greeted a traveler often in this part of central Germany. Hills interspersed with quiet valleys, and rivers meandering through them - some with substantial barge traffic and others serene and quiet with only an occasional boat. Thüringen they called this province - the green heart of Germany.

Sebastian was born here, in Eisenach, a bit to the north of the large Thuringian forest, second only in fame to the Black Forest of southern Baden. He had spent most of his life in the province of Thuringia, with occasional forays outside - once to Denmark, once to Hamburg. He had worked all over in Thuringia, it seemed - in Weimar, in Cöthen, in Arnstadt, in Mühlhausen - but for the last fifteen years or so he called Leipzig his home. It was a little bit to the northeast of Thuringia in the neighboring province of Saxony. Leipzig was a principal city of Saxony, about a day's journey south of Berlin. And the church of St. Thomas, where he was music director, among many other duties, was the leading church of the region and well-known in German Protestant Christendom.

The trip to Frankfurt was one of the longest he had made in a while. He had taken the more northerly, main route to Frankfurt. This faster route was well traveled and led through many important cities and towns of central Germany - almost all of them famous during the Reformation period. Martin Luther had traveled this way many times. The names of the towns along the route rolled through the collective memory of German Protestantism

- Weissenfels, Jena, Weimar, Erfurt, Gotha; then his route ran through the Fulda gap into the province of Franken, then to Fulda and on to Frankfurt.

But on the return trip, he had chosen a more southerly, more scenic and more bucolic route. There was plenty of time, after all, and there was no need to hurry. This route had taken him to Aschaffenburg along the river Main, then over to Lohr, then up a tributary of the river Main, the Saale. They had overnighted in Bad Kissingen, a quaint and lovely town along the river. Now they were approaching Meiningen, on the river Werra, which flowed north into the Weser, always heavy with barge traffic to Bremen, a Hanseatic city and busy center of commerce. Perhaps they could get through the forest and on to Arnstadt for the second overnight. That was the plan anyway.

The stagecoach he had taken left Frankfurt, to the southwest, a day before. This was the second day of a three-day journey, and the coach was approaching the Thuringian Forest from the south and west. The stagecoach crossed a small bridge over a millstream and halted briefly on the other side. The driver motioned to the footman, who dismounted to purchase a newspaper from a stand at a rest station along the way. He moved quickly back to the door of the coach and rapped on the window.

"Herr Bach," he said firmly, "newspaper here. You might wish to read a bit. Esseldingen - about another hour."

"Thank you," he said gratefully, as he carefully retrieved the paper, closed the door and settled in to read. It wasn't much of a paper really, not like the ones in Frankfurt, but it did carry news of more than local interest. It was dated October 14, 1742 - yesterday.

He was not entirely comfortable in the coach, but there was room to move around if he got stiff. And he could change seats to vary the view. He relaxed in the seat, as the coach started up again, and read the headlines - the headlines of Handel's visit to Frankfurt - and the concert he gave there - the one Bach had traveled all this distance from Leipzig to see. Only he hadn't made it. A wheel had fallen off the coach on the way in - right in the middle of nowhere. The repair took two days. That was enough to ruin the trip.

"The opportunity of a lifetime. He is in Germany only once, and the only chance I had ... missed. Bah!" A few stronger words may have escaped Bach's mouth, but his Bible fell from the seat onto the floor in response to a particular bump in the road. "Yes, I know you are in charge, Lord," he mumbled, "but this was very trying, and I will not get a chance like this again - to hear the greatest composer of our age doing his own works. Ach, it's a real pity, and I'm very disappointed. Nevertheless, all things in your hands, Lord."

As he read on, some of Handel's music ran through his head. He tilted his head back and imagined the thrill of the concert, the excited expectations of the audience, the heavenly uplift of magnificent music. It was an historical moment - a concert by a world-renowned musician. Things like this didn't happen every day. And the music ... music much as he himself wrote. Music to glorify God and to edify man - and to lift the human soul. Music to inspire, to console, to rejoice. Yes, it was a special calling to be a composer - a noble profession. Martin Luther was right. Next to theology, music was the most important thing in the world, because music surrounded the throne of God and would forever be.

The newspaper headlines ran past his eyes again and again:

"Handel great success in Frankfurt"

"Large crowds at every performance"

"Superb musical performance"

"Selections from Handel operas create great stir"

He could imagine the selections. Some of the works he knew - only too few. The others - well, they had to be as good - if not better. Handel's writing had such a flair for the dramatic. Something he may have lacked. Possibly, it was Handel's experience with the theater that made him so convincing a dramatist in music. An audience for which he himself had never written. Maybe the time Handel spent in Italy learning the new techniques to communicate emotion had helped him write for the theater. He had heard of these, though he was always too busy to pursue them in any great depth. His art was his life, and there was always something that could be improved or done better. Bach had never left Germany - except once to visit Buxtehude in Denmark when he was a young lad. He had loved it there, and had learned much from the greatest organist then living. But the prospects of becoming involved with Buxtehude's daughter had given him leave. He was not ready for that at that time.

"Selections from new Oratorio *Messiah* rouse audience like lightning."

And now Handel. He could have learned much from Handel, perhaps how to put more drama in his own music. A few years ago, his son, Wilhelm Friedemann, had actually visited Handel when he was in Halle - not too far from Leipzig. And some music had traded hands, so Bach knew some of Handel's works and vice versa. Yes, that moment in *Judas Maccabeus* when "See how the conquering hero comes" changes from small quartet to full choir, ... yes, *that* was really a moment of music.

Handel wrote superbly for the human voice. Something Bach much admired, and thought he did, too. But perhaps there was something he was missing still. Perhaps there would be something of inestimable value he could learn from so great an artist. He had heard bits and pieces of *L'Allegro ed il Penseroso*, including the laughter song, the song of the lark, and the nightingale song – "I woo to hear thine evensong" - yes, especially that. How he had marveled at Handel's use of the human voice as musical instrument. Beautiful, perfect, superbly done. But he had missed the concert. It would likely be the only opportunity in his life for something like that. Of that he was sure.

"Verdammt!" The expletive exploded through clenched teeth. The heat of his frustration erupted without thinking. A pang of remorse struck him immediately. "I'm sorry, Lord," he muttered under his breath. "My anger again. My impatience. My lack of faith in your ways. And maybe my pride. Forgive me. But this was very disappointing."

Anger and impatience. Well, nobody was perfect in this world. He was often frustrated by the inabilities of other people. He never minded those who tried, who made an honest effort. The act of trying was itself something worthy, deserving a measure of respect. And people who had excellence, yes, those he admired and enjoyed working with. It was the dilettantes he hated. And the political types. He remembered the embarrassment that had ensued after he reprimanded the mayor's nephew, a boy who lacked not only talent, but also work ethic. That was probably what had set him off the most. For a German not to have talent was no shame, but for a German to be lazy and indolent - especially in music, and especially with *his* music - well, *that* could not be suffered. That just had to be dealt with. And Bach was not one to mince words.

"You have no talent or interest," he had said to the boy, "so what are you doing here? Why don't you go be a blacksmith?"

His words had been taken as an insult by the uncle, and he had been the one reprimanded - right in front of the Bishop and the Town Council. It was humiliating and very trying. He had had to keep his tongue and give his deference in order to keep his job - which he could not afford to lose with such a large family to support. The shame of it.

Shaking his head, he put down the newspaper; then with a walking stick he banged firmly on the ceiling. That got the drivers' attention. The footman bent down to stare into the interior.

"How far to Klarfeld?" he asked impatiently, sticking his head out the window.

"About fifteen minutes," replied the footman. "Esseldingen next stop after that."

He closed the door window and settled back for a short ride before town. "Aaaahhhh," he sighed. "No sense to worry about it now." Looking out the window he couldn't help noticing the beauty of the scenery. A hawk was circling lazily above, eyeing the coach, and dipping its wings every now and then as it changed direction. The rolling hills and the woods were backdrop to the bird. A forest of trees - lots of them - all green, a beautiful, restful color. Leipzig wasn't quite like this, but it wasn't bad. A nice town ... a big city, really, but it had the flavor of a small town. His work was well defined. Sunday music, a new cantata every week. That could not be expected, even from Bach, but he gave them plenty of new pieces. And then the choir - a good choir. Some excellent singers, his wife being one of the principal sopranos. The church of St. Thomas was no mean place. And the teaching; yes, it could be burdensome at times, but one did have to make a living. And his children took part in everything. That was wonderful. He smiled at the recollections. He loved having children all about. It did get untidy at times, and his wife did get overwhelmed occasionally, but he didn't mind helping out.

He shook his head briefly at the thought that he hadn't been the first choice at St. Thomas. Telemann was the first choice. In a way, he couldn't help agreeing. Telemann's music was the most popular in Germany at the time. Even he liked it, especially the writing for trumpets. Great inventiveness, lively, yet with depth and attraction. Yes, Telemann was a genius ... but not a choir director, and he had turned them down. By the time they got around to it, he had been their third choice - almost the last. He shook his head.

"A mediocrity," they had called him.

"A non-entity."

"St. Thomas deserved better."

Yes, he had his detractors like any person of position, but his stern, Protestant religion had taught him to expect difficulties. The hymn of Martin Luther rang always in his ears – "though this world with devils filled ..." There certainly seemed to be plenty. He bore it all with quiet demeanor - at least most of the time.

He reflected further on St. Thomas'. Perhaps the time he had spent at the secular court in Cöthen had not helped.

Six years and almost no religious works published. And the court was very confining; he could not get permission to leave, and so was virtually unknown outside it. That could have been the reason. But now he had the job at St. Thomas, and he didn't mind. A fine way to serve the Lord his God. Sometimes it just took all he had. It was good to take a trip like this and get away for a little bit. Clear the cobwebs of the mind.

He reached into his bag, almost unconsciously, and retrieved a letter that had been passed on to him by the church elders. He opened it and read the short message. A group of Dutch and German missionaries in Japan had contacted St. Thomas and wanted him to send over some relatively simple music for worship that would be suitable for playing on a small two-rank organ. The letter indicated they would be moving north to the mountains of Japan in more remote locations, one of them being a place called Yonezawa. The elders had asked him to comply. "Well, I should be able to do this," he mused out loud. A few choruses from his Cantatas should help, and a couple of the less complicated organ works might do as well. He mused on a little.

"Klarfeld. Klarfeld here," the coachman interrupted his thoughts, pulling up on the reins and rousing Bach from his reverie. Finally, they were coming into town.

CHAPTER 2

KLARFELD

The coach pulled up slowly to a tavern - a medieval-style, half-timbered structure, quaint, with leaded glass windows. Sebastian took in the view. The white stucco of the building contrasted with the dark beams of heavy wood running up and down and crossways all along the front. A pitcher of overflowing beer was carved on the sign, swinging from a wrought iron stanchion above the door. It announced the name of the tavern - *Zum Krug* - at the pitcher. The sign was painted in a medium blue, contrasting with the white foam of a head of beer and the golden color of the brew itself showing through a glass mug. It did look refreshing and inviting, and he was glad when the coach halted in front. The footman quickly opened the door and dropped the stepping stair with a practiced speed that seemed effortless.

"We'll be here about an hour," the man said. "Take care of the horses and fill our tankards, too. You're welcome to visit."

Sebastian stepped carefully down the stairs, stretched a little to banish the stiffness of the journey and walked slowly towards the tavern. At that, a cleric and parishioner passed by on the street, close to the tavern, and stopped a few feet away. He overheard a snippet of their conversation.

"I was there. Can you believe it?" said the cleric. "Handel was magnificent! The concert was stupendous. The greatest musical celebration I ever heard. Angels could not have sung finer. And that "Messiah." Utterly stupendous - a master work. I will never forget it."

"If only we could have such talent here in Klarfeld once in awhile," replied the parishioner. "Handel is German, no? Could we not make some offer? A concert like that would be the event of a lifetime."

"Well, I think Handel does not get to places like Klarfeld. The English have him now," replied the cleric. "Our George is the king of England, after all. And Handel is very popular. I imagine they pay him well. Much better than we could."

He hesitated a bit before moving on into the tavern, struggling to staunch his disappointment. It took a little time to get used to the low light, as he entered through a heavy oaken door. He took a table in a bit from the door. The waiter was attentive, and the ritual familiar. The beer was good, and he was in the mood for a little refreshment, but a couple of beers over the span of thirty minutes was enough. He made his way out the door and towards the coach.

"Good rest, Herr Bach?" The footman greeted him as he approached.

"Yes. Good beer here, too. Ready for the next leg," he replied.

The footman jumped down off the driving bench, and Sebastian was about to open the door of the coach, when a sudden commotion up the street drew his attention. A pig, squealing raucously, had jumped its owner's cart and taken off towards the carriage. At almost the same time a young boy, about twelve years old, tore off his coat, charged across the street and tackled the pig with obvious pleasure. He held down the squirming animal with a big grin on his face, thoroughly enjoying the moment, as the owner shuffled towards him puffing mightily. His mother, holding the coat, watched in horror from the side of the street.

"Hans! What are you *doing*?" she screamed.

"I got him," Hans yelled back triumphantly.

The pig's owner finally arrived and took control by placing a leash around its neck.

"There, young lad," he puffed. "A great job. Here's a little reward for you."

Hans was grinning broadly as he approached his mother, opening his hand to show two silver coins for his trouble.

"Lunch and dinner," he announced enthusiastically.

The boy's mother was an attractive woman of about thirty-five. Typical north German. Nice blond hair, well-built figure - not exactly slim, but not heavy either. Of medium height, she moved with agility and did not have the manner of a lower class woman. Yet she did not look aristocratic either. Her dress was plain, and her manner without airs, and there was a dignity of bearing, an independence almost, about her.

"Look at you," she said scoldingly. "We have to go home today."

Hans brushed himself off a little embarrassed, still grinning towards his mother.

"Ah, it's nothing," he said. "I'm ready."

They both approached the coach where Sebastian was still standing.

"Well, that was quite a feat, young man," he exclaimed, as they approached. The footman took the baggage from the mother.

"Ah, it was nothing," said Hans matter of factly. "My uncle has a farm here, and I love the animals. Especially the pigs. They are a lot of fun to chase. I got pretty good at it, I guess. Ha!" He moved with athletic ease, his face still smiling with bright blue eyes and tousled blond hair. He exuded the confidence and life of a boy just before puberty.

A year or two would probably change Hans, from an eager, bright-eyed child into an awkward, ungainly and non-communicative youth. *Ach*, what changes life could bring. How could one learn to enjoy the present?

The boy brushed on into the coach ahead of his mother, Sebastian politely deferring to her as she approached.

"Thank you," she said stiffly, looking at him a bit coldly.

He followed her in as the footman closed the door, and they made ready for the journey. The coach interior seemed a lot smaller when he entered. The boy and his mother were facing him on the opposite seat.

"Are you on the way to Jena?" he asked matter of factly, attempting to start some polite conversation.

"No," replied the mother. "We are going to Esseldingen."

"That's where we live," the boy chimed in. "At the *Pension Himmelfreude*. And where are you going?"

"Back to Leipzig," he said tiredly.

"Leipzig," cried the boy. "That is a really big city. Are you the mayor?"

"Hans, that is enough," said the mother firmly. Then to Sebastian she said, "I am Anna Bohlen, and this is my son, Hans."

"Glad to meet you," he responded. "I am Sebastian Bach, a musician by trade. I am the organist at *St. Thomaskirche* in Leipzig. Music teacher, composer, choir director, mechanic, repairman ... I don't know what else I do."

The mother and the boy looked at each other.

"My mom can sing like an angel!" the boy piped up.

"Hans," exclaimed the mother, giving her son a cold stare.

"If that is true, that is certainly nothing to be ashamed of," he offered in return.

"I did sing a lot for the church, before my husband died. Now, I find ... it's hard to do. So I don't." She looked away with a forlorn look for a brief moment. Then her eyes rested on him again. "And where did your journey take you?" she asked, a little curiosity showing.

"Well, I was in Frankfurt," he replied, "that is, almost in Frankfurt. I was on my way to a very special concert - George Frederic Handel - the great composer and organist - the celebrated Saxon. But unfortunately the coach broke down, and ... I, uhh, did not make it in time."

"Oh, too bad," exclaimed Hans. "What a waste of time."

A cold stare from his mother brought the apology.

"I'm sorry," said Hans, lowering his eyes. "I didn't mean to …"

"That's quite all right, young man," Sebastian replied. "A little honesty is often good. It was in fact a waste of time. But I didn't know that in advance. We only live a day at a time, don't we? And it was a great disappointment for me. The only chance I will get in my life to do such a thing. And now, I am on my way home. I feel like I went fishing and came back with nothing. But it's over."

"Oh, I know about that," said Hans, nodding his head. "What kind of instrument do you play?" He asked inquisitively.

"Ah, yes," said Bach, warming to his passion. "I play all kinds of instruments, really, but the organ is my favorite. It's like having a whole orchestra at your fingertips, and," - he smiled a little playfully at Hans – "when I have a full church organ, I can make the building shake."

"Wow. I would like to hear *that*. Wouldn't you, *Mutti*?" Hans looked at his mother enthusiastically, but got only a disinterested "eh" from her. "Our church has an organ - at least, it did have one," he went on. "The organ has the most sounds of anything. But you have to play it with *both* hands and *both* feet. How can anyone do that?"

Sebastian smiled and laughed modestly. "Like a lot of things in life, you cannot do it without long hours of practice and hard work." He looked quizzically at the boy. "You seem to know a lot about music, and you certainly are not shy about asking questions. Do you play an instrument?"

"Of course," said Hans proudly. "I can play the *Blockflöte,* and I am studying the viol. Everyone in Germany can play something." Hans suddenly sat up straight. "Say, if you play the organ, can you fix it, too?"

"Well, I ..." He started his response.

"Hans," Anna jumped in, "you are a lovely boy, but sometimes you talk too much!" She turned her attention to Sebastian. "Herr Bach," she began, as all parents do when they feel their offspring's version lacks certain meaningful detail and subtlety, "our church - in Esseldingen - well, the organ has been broken for about two years now. It's old. We don't have the experts to fix it. The men of the town have tried, but they are not ... well ... they did the best they could - all they could. It was not enough."

"Well, *that* doesn't do much for the worship, does it?" he said quietly. "Hard to worship God without music. What kind was it? Do you know?"

"It was by Hans Schmidt of Hamburg," Hans blurted. "I saw the big brass plaque on the side. He has my name!"

"Well," mused Bach aloud. "I know this organ. Not very many made - and not made anymore. Some problems with tracking rods, I seem to remember."

"Can you fix it then?" Hans piped up again.

"Well, I don't know," he said carefully. "I haven't seen it." He hesitated. "It could be a very big job. I don't have a lot of time."

"I think the church would pay," said Anna. "Maybe it would not be so much. We are a village parish, after all. But they really would love to have it fixed." She looked at him with curiosity in her eyes. Maybe it was more than just curiosity. "And I would like to hear you play," she said quietly. "Music does mean a lot in Germany. Not to have it is like to go without dinner - and that would make a man very thin and very unhappy. I am sure the congregation would love to have *someone* fix it."

"Well, even to look at it would obligate me. I am already in difficulty with my employers over this trip. I don't think I could do that. It could take weeks. No, impossible." He shook his head emphatically.

"But you may never get a chance like this again!" Anna said boldly. "Restoring music to its rightful place in worship - that would make so many people happy. You would be appreciated forever, and God would be well pleased. Don't you think?"

He was being drawn into this, he sensed, but he was not in the mood to be convinced. He had come up empty on his little trip, a trip he had had to ask permission to go on. And now that he was coming back without actually having *heard* Handel or met him, ... well, his employers wouldn't look on that with much favor. A delay on top of that could make him look bad, a dereliction of duty.

But, on the other hand, wasn't this what ministry was all about? He could do it ... really ... probably. Just take some time. And what would his employers think? What of his wife and children back in Leipzig? Hmmmm. They were expecting him shortly. A long delay could be a problem, but fixing a church organ would give him a good reason for the delay and explain his missed concert. It could not take too long; maybe ... he should do it.

But to take that kind of time out of his busy schedule? Didn't he have that new Cantata to finish, and the Oratorio for Christmas? And what of that new tenor to train? And what about those letters of recommendation to write for his students who were seeking employment - his own son being one of them? *Ach* ... to cater to anyone who wanted their instrument repaired, well, that wasn't what he was called to do, was it? There were so many other important tasks to do that *were* his calling, he could not stop to entertain everyone's needs, could he?

The coach pulled to a stop interrupting his thoughts. He looked out the window half paying attention and saw nothing. Then a feeling crept over him. Could it be brigands holding up their progress? They were known sometimes in Germany - robbing coaches and passengers. Travel was not the safest activity in the world. He rolled down the window and stuck his head out the door, addressing the footman.

"Why are we stopped?" he asked, a little upset.

"We are coming into the county of the Duke of Wetzlar. Have to pay a toll, *Zuschlag* - a little extra for your protection. All adult passengers will be assessed. Not too much - eighth of a *Thaler* - three *Groschen* - per person. The official will be here in a minute."

"Ahhh, money," he sighed quietly as he sat back in the seat, leaving the window down. He reached for some change, motioning to the others that he would handle it. The world revolved around money - too much, it seemed. Sometimes the dukes placed chains across rivers that handled major barge traffic. They raised the chains so that the ship could not pass until it paid the toll. The tolls were irksome, but not extravagant. Everybody had to live somehow. And it did deter bandits.

So did firearms. The footman had a blunderbuss, and the coachman two pistols - not a lot to deter a large band of brigands, but enough to discourage the general practice. No one else could own a firearm, unless he was a hunter. So only the police and travel professionals had them outside of the military. Oh yes, brigands never had trouble getting such weapons. That certainly gave one pause.

And the cousin of brigandage was tyranny. Ha! The subject was a serious one, but tyranny could not rise in Germany. Impossible. The political system saw to that. The Holy Roman Empire of the German Nation. Every level of aristocracy had its authority. Every principality had its ruler. The Emperor could do little, really. It was a democratic system of sorts - for the rulers, not for the people. But it worked.

The French had laughed. "It wasn't holy, it wasn't Roman, and it wasn't an empire."

But Germans were always involved in some argument that needed resolution somewhere, so the officials were kept busy. And Germany was not really a country - a people to be sure, a state of being maybe, but a country with a king, no. That prospect was frightening to too many people, including the French, so the Empire system continued - a decentralized, semi-democratic, divided land.

But it was a Christian land and a free land. They had Martin Luther to thank for that. Yes, the wars of the last century lasting nearly thirty years had almost depopulated Germany. What an awful affair that had been. Diseases had killed more people than the soldiers had. But now, Germany had returned to normalcy, with a new tolerance for religious differences. The population had largely recovered, and they were still strongly Christian. For that he was deeply grateful. There was a kind of peace, and he had a job and a calling. No tyrant would raise his head in Germany. That would be impossible.

"Six *Groschen*, please," rang out the toll-taker's voice at the window.

Sebastian reached into his pocket and handed over the change waving away the silent protestations of the boy and his mother.

As the coach started up again, he leaned back in his seat. It seemed like the others were talked out for the time being, so he began to think about his life to this point. His early years had been difficult, very difficult. He was orphaned at an early age. His mother had died when he was nine and his father shortly thereafter. He had been brought up in the household of his older brother, a kind man, but not a musician.

Yet, the Bach family name boasted of many musicians - all over central Germany. They were composers, *Kapellmeister* (band leaders, conductors), court musicians, singers, builders of instruments, and participants in various and sundry activities related to music in some way. It was no accident that music was his life. It was a clear appointment given to him by God Almighty. That was what he believed, and he shook his head thinking about his life mission - to glorify God through music.

Only, it hadn't been easy. He had attended school to graduation, and of that he was grateful. Then nearly twenty and looking for a job, he landed a position as organist at the court of the Duke of Saxe-Weimar - after he had been summarily dismissed from his first position. That duke did not take a liking to him, and he had held the position for the princely duration of one day. He had then worked in Arnstadt for a few years, then on to Mühlhausen for a brief stay. The Arnstadt people had not been pleased with his "independent spirit," as they called it. But in Mühlhausen he had gotten along well with the authorities and had met and married a cousin, Maria Barbara.

Family had come along quickly, and he had then taken a bigger job in Weimar, where he remained for almost ten years. And his family grew. Higher salaries beckoned, and he moved to a princely court at Cöthen. He stayed six years at Cöthen, and had always had good relationships there. But Maria Barbara had died there, and a few years later, he had married again - to a wonderful singer, a soprano of professional stature, Anna Magdalena Wilcke, and she had borne him more children.

And now he was in Leipzig - for quite some time. It was good. He was doing what he loved. Composing, teaching, leading performances, making the acquaintance of highly placed people - dukes, kings, and leaders in the church. His family was well taken care of, and they had many great opportunities for growing up and developing - especially in music. There was never a dull moment. There were always guests coming and going, students to teach - and to help place when they graduated. Four of his sons were serious musicians and composers. Twenty children in all, he mused with a wry smile.

Then the smile turned down when he recalled that only half had survived to adulthood. Life was hard. There had been plagues, diseases, accidents, and fevers. A serious cut on the body could be life threatening. Medical care was not common. Sometimes the quality of the food or the water was not what it should be. The first few years of childhood were especially trying - not much in the way of medical guidance or equipment for vulnerable, little babies. There had been plenty of confrontations with the grim reaper. His soul had agonized over that with many others having the same experience. They had cried out to God for mercy and healing. Only it hadn't happened. Survival was triumph enough, it seemed. They needed to thank God for that - that half had survived - and leave the rest to Him.

He looked over at Hans briefly. The boy reminded him of his little Carl - so enthusiastic and energetic. Good health and cheerful disposition was such a blessing.

And Anna? He studied her face discreetly. It was youthful still, beautiful, with a lovely complexion, but the sadness of her loss showed in a cold, defensive, cautious demeanor. He wondered about her singing and thought of the special character a good soprano brings to the music of worship. How special his own wife was to him - personally as well as professionally. It was sad to see such talent unused, thwarted in the service of God. Could that change? He mused on, slowly drowsing off into a comfortable sleep.

CHAPTER 3

YAMAGATA

Late afternoon the coach pulled into town slowly. The creaking wheels and the gentle swaying roused Bach from his sleepy rest. But what town was this? As Sebastian awoke and looked out the window, his eyes beheld the strangest sights. Rice paddies. The houses had upturned edges to the roof. Ox carts. There were people in kimonos and strange dress. The town was strange, too. Houses and buildings with oiled paper windows on wooden frames. But there, over there, it looked like a tavern, and there a livery, a square, a marketplace - and a little farther down the main street stood a small building with a steeple and ... a cross. Was it a church?

He looked over at where the other passengers had sat. They had already departed. A quick look up the street showed a woman with a boy of about twelve years, but they did not look like Anna and Hans. She had jet-black hair and wore a full kimono, and the boy, also dark haired, had on a white, loose fitting jacket and pants.

He opened the door and cried out, "Anna!"

The woman turned. "Hana-ko, *Koku-jin*." She smiled and bowed. "Hanzu, you too!" The boy bowed also.

What a strange tongue, but he understood it perfectly. How could that be? It was a wonder, no doubt. But what should he make of it?

"Where are we?" He asked.

"In Yamagata. Where we are going. Didn't we tell you? We are going to the Inn of Happiness, where we live. Don't you remember? Were you asleep so long?"

The inn was up the street a bit, the sign, swaying slightly in the breeze. It was quaint and a bit romantic, but built in an architectural style he had never seen before. Beyond the houses of the town, fields stretched to the distant hills dotted with small houses. Rice paddies everywhere, vegetable plots here and there. Some cattle, pigs and chickens occupied the yards and the fields. What strange land was this?

People went their way past the coach busily engaged in the labor of life - butchers, farmers, cabinetry workers, brewers, tradesmen of various kinds. Some carts carrying produce and cloth rumbled past at a deliberate pace. Nothing rushed. No stress and hubbub of a city like Leipzig.

"Where am I?" he asked.

"In Japan, of course. We are on Honshu, the main island, but in the north, in the mountains. This is where we live. Yonezawa. Isn't it beautiful?" Hana-ko replied. "Didn't we tell you? We asked you to come, and you said yes."

Then Sebastian stepped out of the coach. Just as his foot hit the ground, the axle hub gave a creaking groan, and the wheel leaned directly against the carriage. The footman looked up at the coachman sitting up high on the driver's bench. A rapidly moving, small shadow of a hawk flitted across them both.

"Not again," the driver exclaimed.

"I'm afraid the axle is broken this time," responded the footman. "This could take a week to fix."

"Oh, for goodness sake," the driver replied a bit peevishly. Turning to Sebastian he said, "well, we will have to break your ticket, Herr Bach. Pick you up again in ... a week?" The coachman explained.

"Maybe a week," he replied hesitantly, " ... or two. It appears I will be staying for a little while."

The coachman nodded. "No trouble. We know who you are, and we know where you'll be." Then the man added, a little apologetically, "Very sorry about the breakdown that caused you to miss your appointment."

"Not your fault," he replied Bach gamely. "You did the best you could. I'll be looking for you."

"Thank you." The coachman waved. "We'll be there. *Wiedersehen.*"

There was something cheerful in the coachman's "goodbye" in spite of the circumstances. Friendly people did help to make a trip more pleasant. It did something for one's state of mind. But to wind up here?

As the coach limped slowly away, he waved and turned to find his two companions.

"It appears I will be staying after all," he offered sheepishly.

But they were already moving towards the inn and were busily talking to a few people who had come up around them. One of them, talking to Hana-ko, was dressed in a black clerical frock and had a soft, flat and floppy, four-cornered hat on his head that seemed to signify some kind of authority and position. Gold tassels hung from each corner. He was an older man, a bit taller than most and relatively slender with dark hair mixed with gray.

"But we can't have any idiot work on this instrument," said the rector testily. "Look at what the others have done. And who is this *Koku-jin*? I have never heard of him. How do we know he can fix his own pants?"

Sebastian took a long, deep breath, rolled his eyes a bit and walked slowly into the conversation.

"Oh, *Koku-jin*," exclaimed Hana-ko, "this is Rector Uetake of our church. I was ..."

"Well, *Koku-jin*," said the rector in a businesslike and bothered way, "organ repair is a very serious undertaking - not for journeymen. The instrument is over fifty years old and needs the care of an expert. Are you sure you can fix it?"

"Well, I *am* a church organist," he said, looking the rector in the eye, calmly.

"That doesn't mean you are a repairman," interrupted the rector a little testily.

"Yes, in general you are right," he replied a little tiredly, "but I was a student of Buxtehude, and I have fixed many instruments in my day." He engaged the rector with arched eyebrows, as if to put him in his place. "Yours is not the first that needs repair."

"Nor the last, no doubt," replied the rector with no little pique. "And who is Buxtehude?"

A face from the small crowd thrust itself forward.

"We don't need another idiot fooling around with the organ. We just need the right materials, and we can do it. There is no mystery to this organ." It was Matsui-san, the village apothecary. Of medium height and build, he had dark black hair and a smooth complexion. He wore an agitated expression on his face and had dark, intense eyes.

It was the rector's turn to take a big breath. "Yes, Matsui-san," he responded evenly, "in general, you are right." Then, turning from Sebastian to the apothecary, "but we have been without it too long, not to try *something*, at least." He turned back slowly. "Well, what credentials do you have, *Koku-jin,* for this kind of job?" His voice betrayed a calmer resignation.

"I have repaired these organs in the past," he replied plainly.

"But where are his papers?" Matsui-san insisted. "With whom did you apprentice? Who is this Buxtehude? Did he know how to fix the instrument? You must be a master to do such things. Some child off the street cannot do it."

Sebastian bristled at the slur, his eyes narrowing sharply.

"Matsui-san," replied the rector a bit tiredly, "I am inclined to let him try, at least. To do nothing is to do worse."

"He'll get no support from me," replied Matsui-san disgustedly. "We only need to wait until we can get the right materials. All the guilds agree with me."

"These materials are expensive, and we have waited too long already," said the rector emphatically. "*Koku-jin,* how long do you anticipate this will take?"

"I don't know without seeing the instrument," he responded. "I don't know who makes the parts anymore. What was really the problem?"

"Too many for you to solve," spit out Matsui-san.

He shot a glance at Matsui-san, his temper rising. With an effort to control his tongue, he replied, "It probably wouldn't help if people were the problem in addition."

"You couldn't do it in a month, if you had the whole town to help." Matsui-san snorted, as he turned sharply and walked away.

The crowd slowly dispersed except for Hana-ko, Hanzu, and another man. Sebastian picked up his bags and turned to go.

"*Koku-jin,* a word please?" The man came over quietly and stopped him.

"Yes?" He turned.

"I am Uesugo - a cabinetmaker in town. I have seen the organ and tried to help. Matsui-san is a difficult man to deal with, but he is right. We were able to fix only the simplest problems. You are not likely to get much cooperation from him or his friends. If you wish, though, I would like to help."

"Why, thank you," he replied gratefully. "Why is it that you are of such a different opinion than the rest?"

Uesugo's face wore the expression of a kind and patient man. "I love the music of the organ. And I know with love, all things are possible."

"Thank you. That is very kind," he returned, though taken a little aback. "In fact I have repaired organs before, and I know what some of the problems are. They can be difficult to fix. But please come tomorrow. I would be interested to know all that you have experienced."

"We have experienced mostly failure," responded Uesugo. "It has been frustrating and disappointing, and for those of us who love music, it has been a little bit lonely and sad."

"I will do what I can," he said.

They bowed and shook hands. Uesugo departed, and Sebastian took up his bags again to go. The streets had quieted.

"*Koku-jin,* where will you stay?" Hana-ko interrupted.

"I will find a room," he replied. A tavern up the street beckoned.

"Why don't you stay with us?" Hanzu blurted out.

"Hanzu!" Hana-ko scolded the boy. Then turning to Sebastian, she said, "we have a room in the Inn of Happiness, upstairs. They have another room downstairs, which I think is free; and in the lobby there is a clavichord. I think it would do well enough. No?"

"That would be very well, very well indeed," he said brightening. "And for dinner?"

"We have a small restaurant off the lobby. It's more home-style cooking, but the food is well prepared." She smiled. "And there is plenty of it. We don't get too many travelers coming through here, but those who do often stay at the inn." Hana-ko picked up her bag. "Are you ... ?"

"Yes, of course," he replied before she could finish. He shuffled his bags, holding them a little awkwardly, as they all turned to go towards the Inn of Happiness.

CHAPTER 4

THE ORGAN

In the morning, after a nice breakfast of dried salmon, rice and tea, Sebastian slowly opened the front door of the inn leading to the street and stepped out into a light mist. Hanzu followed sleepily. He smiled as he held the door for the boy. Hanzu was at that age when getting up early to eagerly wake up his mother snoozing in her bed ... was past him.

The cobblestones were hard and wet, as he and the boy moved up the street to the church. The church building was made partly of stone, built about a hundred years ago. It was fairly sizable by the standards of the town, but not really large like a cathedral. It was a rectangular structure with larger windows than most of the surrounding buildings. The roof was sharply angled, and the steeple in the front was off center a bit.

Sebastian pushed open one of the large oak double doors at the entrance. Inside, it was quiet and a little dark, some light streaming through the windows on the eastern side.

"Hmmmm. Very nice wood," he murmured, as he surveyed the pews, the walls, the altar, and the lectern.

Wooden choir benches faced each other behind the altar. The organ pipes were arranged above the console off to the left of the chancel. As they approached the organ keyboard from the center aisle, a figure was already waiting there. It was Uesugo.

"Ohayo gozimasu," he said quietly.

Sebastian and the boy nodded a "good morning" in return, as they came up to him.

He went right to the console and looked it over. It was dusty from lack of use. A few slats were broken, and some keys were missing. His eyes slowly moved across the structure to the brass plaque on the right side.

Hans Schmidt, Hamburg 1685, it said.

He motioned to Uesugo briefly; then they both lifted the top cover of the instrument.

"Wow." Hanzu whispered in amazement as he took in the scores of rows of key slats and their connections to the tracker rods. The complexity overwhelmed him.

Sebastian studied the layout carefully; then he pressed a few keys to test the action. Some stuck, others depressed easily - too easily. This indicated something was broken inside.

"This will take some work," he said quietly, mostly to himself, but loud enough for the others to hear. "Maybe not too much though."

The organ had two manuals (keyboards) and a pedal board - typical for medium-sized organs of the day. One keyboard for the *Hauptwerk* (Great organ), one for the *Brustwerk* (the equivalent of the modern Swell organ) and one for the *Rückpositiv* (an organ division placed usually behind the organist's bench). Only there was no *Rückpositiv*, really. These pipes had been placed above with all the rest in a kind of *Oberwerk* (higher manual).

"Hmmm," he mused aloud.

The organ had only these three divisions - typical for this size church. In Leipzig he had four. He then ran his hands over the stop buttons and tried pulling a few. Some moved too easily, and a few did not move at all. Stuck.

"We have some real problems here," he spoke more seriously, as he went through all twenty-six stop knobs. "We are going to have to take a look at the air chamber and the pipe chests."

They all moved behind the console and went through a door that led them up to the air chamber room. He stopped a few paces into the small, cramped room as the others followed in behind him. He looked around the room slowly at all of the guts of the machine, quite familiar, and a little comforting. In the back a little was the large wind chest to hold the air pressure, the double pedal wheels and bellows for the pedalers, the ones who actually produced the air pressure by working bellows by means of a foot crank. Large diameter wooden tubes connected by leather hoses took the air to the pipe chests of the three divisions of the organ.

"I had no idea it takes all this to make a sound," whispered Hanzu, having followed him closely into the room.

"It looks to me that some work is also needed here," he said. "Let's go up and look at the pipes." They all moved carefully out of the room, into the chancel area, then up some back stairs to the pipe loft. They moved around slowly and carefully, examining the pipes and the wind chests they sat in.

In each pipe chest were stop slides to get the tone desired by sounding only the pipes of that rank when a key was pressed. The slides had holes in them to carry that out. Pulling a stop knob moved the slide, so the holes lined up with the pipes. Pressing a key on the console opened the air channel to a particular pipe to get a note. Some stops sounded in combinations by moving several slides rather than one.

He noted the ranks, the sizes, the quality of the pipes. He stepped up on a small catwalk and picked off a smaller, stopped pipe and blew into it gently. It was off key, and he adjusted it on the spot by moving the metal "hat" or stop on the large end back and forth until he found the right note.

"It's going to need some tuning, too." His eyes moved to engage Hanzu. "That's where you can help."

"Me?" Hanzu replied, a little taken aback. "What can I do?" Then pointing to the pipe he still held in his hand, the boy said, "How did you do that? Set the pipe note, I mean."

He smiled. "It was out of tune. The wrong note. A little flat. Things like this happen all the time."

"But how do you know it's right now?" Hanzu asked quizzically.

The boy could have no idea Sebastian was the perfecter of the well-tempered system, where all instruments were tuned to the same notes of equal intervals of the scale instead of playing in their natural keys, all of which were slightly different from each other. This one system made ensemble playing a harmonious occasion and opened up the world of harmony in music. Some had complained that specific instruments had lost their individuality, and some said all the intervals were out of tune except the octave and the unison. But it seemed to most that the gains far outweighed the difficulties, and nothing was out of tune so badly that it could be noticed, except by an expert with a very sensitive ear. And only then, if the note were held for a longer time. A keyboard instrument could now play with any other kind of instrument with this standard tuning method, and the possibilities were endless.

"Up here," he smiled again, pointing to his head, "It's my whole life. After a while you get to know all the notes by heart." But he was being overly modest. It wasn't everybody that had perfect pitch and who knew every note at first hearing.

"I will need you to tune these," he said to Hanzu, indicating the pipes with a sweep of his hand, "while I play on the keys. You are small and young. This would be a very hard job for a man of my age."

"You mean I can crawl in there?" Hanzu looked at the ranks of pipes, and the thrill of a new adventure shone brightly in his dark eyes. "That could be fun! Even up there? Up top?" He indicated the largest pipes. "It would be like the top of a mountain. Are you sure? What if my mother ..."

"Yes, it will be fine," replied Sebastian. "Very safe. We will build you a platform."

"But I see this is more serious than Matsui-san led one to believe," he said, changing the subject. He pulled on a few stop slides on one of the pipe chests. They didn't budge. "Hmm, warpage," he muttered. Then he turned to Uesugo. "Uesugo, is there someone who can work leather in town? Someone that would be willing to help?"

"No," replied Uesugo, "not in this town. But I know someone in Yamashiro who could, if he is not too busy. Do you think that will be enough?"

"No," he replied. "We will need someone who can stitch leather, and someone who can make glue."

"Well." A quiet sigh escaped Uesugo's lips. "Matsui-san, the apothecary, was able to make a decent glue from chemical stores he had in his shop. I don't know if he would be in the mood to help now, though, yet going outside might anger him further. But there are some apprentices in town who are willing and could be taught." He shot a quick look at Sebastian, "if there were someone to teach them."

"Could you?" He asked.

"For wood, yes; for leather, perhaps," responded Uesugo slowly.

"The hoses and the bellows need to be sewn very tightly and glued," he went on intently. "The smaller parts of leather can be tacked firmly. This is the most important job. I can show you how. Can you do it?"

"I believe so." Uesugo responded quietly.

"Some of the slides are stuck - in fact quite a few," he continued. "Wrong thickness or swollen wood or shrunken chest top, or sloppy re-gluing job. We will have to remove the chest tops and see. We will have to check every slide, and I think new tops will have to be made. The wood needs to be well seasoned. Do you have such on hand?"

"Yes, I have plenty," the man replied. "I will have to make up the top from boards I have in stock. That will only take a day. If we need to make cuts, it will take a little longer."

"All right. Let's look at the rods," he said, as he led them all back down to the console.

"Not very pretty, I'm afraid," interjected Uesugo.

"Hmmmm." He picked up a split tracker rod. "The slide must have stuck in the chest, and forcing the rod broke it. What did Matsui-san want?"

"Other than the hand of Hana-ko," replied Uesugo with raised eyebrows, "he proposed oak, but that is rare in this part of Japan."

The hand of Hana-ko? Sebastian caught his breath. Life was getting more complicated.

"Oak is good for the rod, but not the slide," he replied to Uesugo in a steady voice. He held up the rod to the growing light of morning. The chests were of spruce. "If the slide is of a wood too different, moisture can swell it and freeze it in place - and if it is forced at that time - it's almost like gluing it in place forever. Do you have fir? Or spruce?" He looked at Uesugo. "Or good straight pine - no knots?"

"Yes, on all counts." Uesugo took the rod and turned it over in his hands. "I don't remember how much, or of what sizes," he replied. "I will have to check."

"We will have to remove the tops of the pipe chests and probably remake some of the slides. Can you do it?" He lifted his head in Uesugo's direction.

"How many?" Uesugo asked.

"Could be twenty, could be forty. Won't know until we look deeper," he replied.

"In a few days?" Uesugo queried.

"Yes. Do you have the help?"

"I think I can get it. I am not the only shop in town. Perhaps one or two others could help."

"I think the rods should be easy to replace. The actions look to be in good shape, but I will have to test each one. So I think the biggest problems are the slides and the leather seals for the bellows and windpipes. The slides need to be waxed; all moving parts need to be waxed. The pipes themselves look to be in good shape, and the keyboard is mostly sound. I can fix that fairly easily." He took a deep breath and then said, "Well. Let's get started."

"Right now?" Hanzu queried

"Of course," he replied. "No time to waste. But we cannot do everything at once. Let's hope we can find somebody to help."

Hanzu and Uesugo walked slowly out of the church, as Sebastian turned to the altar and paused, looking up at the pipes and taking in the mood of the sanctuary.

This is where people come to worship God, he thought quietly. *And music should be here.* He looked around slowly at the church. It had a stone floor and stone block walls, dark wooden pews and dark roof beams with hanging lanterns. The woodwork was well done. He smiled. A fine Japanese skill. The stone was a grey color, a little somber and plain. It did not have the decoration, charm or color of St. Thomas. The altar area was raised, a lectern serving as the pulpit standing out on the left side as one faced the altar. There was an altar rail up front, the two sides separated by a few stairs in the middle that led up to the choir loft. The organ pipes were all on the left side, and the console was situated below the lectern, off to the left a bit. The place was quiet and peaceful.

He absent-mindedly walked over to the console and sat down. Many of the stops were marked. The *Hauptwerk* division had a *Quintäton*, sixteen feet - the largest pipe of the division. A quick look at the others showed almost the same. There was an eight-foot *Gedackt* in the *Oberwerk* and two sixteen-footers in the *Pedal* - a *Prinzipal* flute pipe and a *Posaune* reed pipe giving a mellow, trombone-like sound. The shortest pipes were the two-footers, one a *Gemshorn* basic flute pipe and another a *Nachthorn* reed pipe. There were several mixtures in all three divisions. But how did they get a German organ here in Japan?

The organ was not too shabby. Typical of what he had played years ago in Weimar and Arnstadt. Only a few reed stops. This was common for German instruments of the day. Most of the pipes were flue pipes, or Diapason, where the sound was made by air passing through a narrow space into an opening and then cut by a flat portion of the pipe on the other side of the opening - much like a whistle or set of Pan pipes. French organ builders were using more reed pipes, which generated sound by vibrating a small, thin metal sheet by air passing over it - much in the same way as a modern clarinet or other orchestral reed instrument. This expanded the capabilities of the organ to give more orchestral sounds. But it did not catch on quite so quickly in Germany.

It was about noon when Sebastian returned to the church, where he now addressed a small crowd of artisans near the console, a group that Uesugo had managed to cobble together. He greeted them briefly and reviewed what he thought would be necessary, then he gave them a brief tour of the workings of the organ.

"All right," he said, "I think you have a good idea what kind of work we need to do. I know this was tried before, but we cannot do it that way again. These organs are very sensitive to tracking rods breaking. We will have to make some new ones. The most important thing for now is the console repair and the wind production. Without that, we are lost. Two days?"

"A week would be more like it," grumbled the first artisan. "We have other work, you know."

"I cannot twiddle my thumbs for so long," he said struggling to control his impatience. "And I cannot stay forever," he snorted. "Forget the other work. We concentrate on this now - ja? The church will pay."

"We've been here before," said a second artisan. "Already tried this. Didn't work." He looked at Sebastian with no little doubt and scorn. "And what makes you think you can do any better?"

"I have done repair work all my life," he replied. "The Hans Schmidt organ is quite sensitive and difficult to repair." He eyed the second artisan coldly. "Maybe you know that now."

"Only too well," interjected the first artisan, hastening to defuse the situation.

The artisans looked at each other, unsure of what to think.

"We must try again," he interjected, softening a little. "We cannot give up. Is this not the Lord's house? Come, no mean effort here. We want excellence. By God's grace we shall have it. But it will take some work. You are not afraid, are you? Come, this has been a wreck long enough. Let us fix this once and for all."

The men turned to go, some of them mumbling, others with a renewed sense of possibility. He could only hope that his exhortation had been enough of a goad to get them to work with purpose and commitment.

CHAPTER 5

MUSIC MAKER

The Inn of Happiness was a nice, quiet place for dinner. Sebastian was seated with Hanzu and Hana-ko at a table in the small dining room. It overlooked the street, now empty and calm. Most people had already taken dinner. The kitchen was behind the dining room and was separated from it by a large double door, through which the servant girl came and went. There were ten tables in the room, all relatively small, seating four at each. A few of the tables were occupied. The dining room was mostly for the inn occupants, but it served the general public as well. The tables and chairs, not too finely finished, were made of sturdy wood that he did not recognize. They were nicely set with plates and bamboo sticks. Some had small, woven cloths on them, too fine to be called a mat, too short to be a tablecloth. There was a counter at the far end, manned by a relative of the owner. The room was reasonably well lit, with candles at every table and hanging lanterns spaced throughout the room. Several windows gave light during the day.

"Well, I must say, I am not used to eating like this," he exclaimed, holding up the chopsticks. "Don't you have a knife and fork?"

"The cook uses those," replied Hana-ko. "We have a *supuun*, though, for the soup."

"The soup is quite delicious," he said, as he sipped from the ceramic creation she had called a spoon. "What is it made of?"

"This is *Miso* soup," Hana-ko went on. "It is the *shiro* or white variety - made from soybeans. It was a royal creation invented by the head cook for the Shogun of Japan many years ago. It became so popular that now we all eat it. You like?"

"Yes, very much. What are the greens?"

"Seaweed."

He raised his eyebrows. "And the lumps? They taste like dumplings - something we eat in Germany a lot."

"Those are *tofu* - made from soybean paste."

He finished the soup just as the main dish was brought in. The food was served in a square tray - not on a plate. The tray was lacquered and molded into compartments, each holding a different food. In one compartment, there were what looked like limp salad greens, and in another, something that looked like a paste. A generous helping of rice came in a bowl on the side. One compartment contained raw meat.

"Do you cook the meat?" He asked.

"Sometimes," replied Hana-ko. We use a *hibachi* - a small wood fire right on the table. You cook yourself and then eat right away. Delicious. This is the best area in Japan for beef."

"We don't eat much beef in Germany. The cows are too valuable for milk and cheese. Mostly we eat pork and fish."

"Ah, in Japan, we don't eat cheese - or drink milk."

"Amazing how different other countries can be," he allowed. "I have never been in a foreign land - except Denmark, but that was hardly foreign. We are not used to eating meat that is not cooked."

"It is all right. We are scrupulously clean in Japan. Water is plentiful and we wash always. Go ahead and try. It is good."

"What kind of meat is it?"

"Horse."

He gagged. The horse did not have a cloven hoof. In European culture eating horse was a sign of starvation. But he didn't want to insult his hosts. So he took a piece and carefully dipped it in the sauce of another compartment on the tray ... and ate. It had a soft, chewy consistency and a delicate flavor. It was a little strange, but did not taste so bad.

He moved to take some green colored paste from one of the other trays. As he put it in his mouth, he asked, "What is thi ..." Before he could finish, his mouth was on fire. He swallowed as quickly as he could, but that made it worse. He choked and gagged, and tears streamed from his eyes. He grabbed the cup of tea and gulped hard, finishing the cup in a few swallows. Catching his breath, and wiping the sweat from his brow, he murmured, "My God. What was that?"

"Wasabi sauce," replied Hana-ko. "It is a condiment - like mustard. Only it is made from a root. I think you call it horseradish. It can be quite hot and spicy, so only take a little." Her advice had come too late.

He then tried a thin, whitish vegetable. It too was spicy, but not hot.

"Pickled ginger," offered Hana-ko. "You like? It goes with the *sushi*, there." She indicated another compartment on the tray. It held three cylindrically shaped rice balls wrapped in a dark, leafy material.

"It is mostly rice, wrapped in seaweed. It has some fresh, raw vegetable and raw fish or other meat. Try it. Use only a little wasabi with it. Delicious. We often have that for lunch. The cooks are very proud of their ability to make it with such a variety of things. They vie with each other for inventiveness. So it is never boring, and always there is rice. It is very common in Japan."

Sebastian asked for more tea, and as the meal finished up, conversation turned to the events of the day.

"And he tuned it right - just like that." Hanzu's voice broke into the quiet exchanges. "I never saw anyone do anything like that."

"The pipe was a little out of tune. Things like that happen all the time," he replied modestly.

"Can you play the clavichord?" Hana-ko interrupted, as she looked at him expectantly.

"Well, of course," he answered, glad for the change in subject. He pushed back from the chair and moved toward the instrument, on the opposite side of the room from the counter. It was located right near a set of stairs that led up to the second and third floors.

Then, almost at the instrument, he hesitated, stopped, turned around and said, "But I will need some help." He smiled a little mischievously at Hanzu, who gave him a quizzical look, not knowing what to expect. "Here, Hanzu. You sit here," he said, indicating the bench at the keyboard.

They both moved to sit down. Sebastian spread his hands over the keys.

"Now," he said to Hanzu, "when I nod my head, you play this note." He indicated the key to him. "Two times - like so." Bom-bom.

Hanzu tried. "Like that?" he asked, his head turning to Sebastian, uncertainty in his young eyes.

"Just like that." He smiled. "But not until I let you know. All right?"

Hanzu nodded.

He began to play the *Minuet in G* - a lovely, lilting piece - do re me sooo - me sooo, do do

He went through the melody twice looking at Hanzu each time for the "do, do." Then he smiled his thanks and went on to play the rest of the piece.

It took all of two minutes or so. Hana-ko seemed surprised and charmed at the simplicity of the piece. Yet it had vigor and tune. He always loved the effect it had on children. The accentuated rhythm and lilting melody made it almost a dance. The rising figures were enough to make one smile.

"That was wonderful!" she exclaimed in a hushed voice, clapping her hands quietly. "A delight. So simple, so ... charming."

"Thank you," he replied. "I wrote that for my family. We always have a lot of fun with that. My sons play with me regularly. Such a pleasure when some in your own family love the same things you do." He and Hanzu approached the table again. Affectionately he tousled Hanzu's hair a little. "I have twelve children and more on the way," he said fondly.

"Twelve?" Hana-ko exclaimed suddenly, a look of almost shock on her face. "My goodness," she continued, calming down a little. "And your wife?"

He sat down at the table slowly. After taking a breath he replied evenly, "My first wife died when I was about your age." He looked at her carefully. "She was the mother of the first seven. I've since remarried, and more children have come along."

Hana-ko looked stunned. She hesitated, her mouth agape. She took a short breath. "I'm sorry. I did not know," she mumbled. "I ..." She gave him a quick look. She started to tear up, then stood up suddenly. "Excuse me, I ..." she barely got the words out, then moved quickly out of the room and up the stairs.

He watched her go, unsure of what to do or say. Had it been something he said?

"Hey, that was really fun." Hanzu broke the mood. "Can you show me more? How did you write that? How did you play it without the music?"

"Well," he replied, "maybe tomorrow we can find out. But now, I think you and your mother need a good night's sleep." He patted the boy fondly on the head, as Hanzu moved from the table to follow his mother up the stairs.

Still perplexed by Hana-ko's strange reaction, he hesitated a bit, then slowly got up and moved to his own room.

As Hana-ko prepared Hanzu's bed for the night, she wondered if Sebastian knew how she felt, or understood. A wave of reminiscence passed over her. She remembered how Hanzu had come into the world. How fearful she had been for her life. The first child was always the most difficult, the midwife had said. It had scared her, as it was not uncommon for women to die in childbirth. Her anxious prayers had been for Hanzu to be a normal delivery. And how supportive her husband, Takash, had been. How she had loved the touch of her husband at that time - and the sound of his voice. Her heart skipped a beat.

Takash had been a strong man, a noted practitioner of *karate* - the Japanese art of self-defense using no weapons. He was not a man of words, though he could be tender at times. But he was always calm - and strong - a tower of strength. How she loved those sculpted, muscled arms. There was power, but gentleness, too. They were arms that cradled her many times in quiet, firm affection. Some times they had softened her anger - other times her fears. He had always been slow and soft with her, even when she lost her composure. That was Takash - like an ox. He was a farmer with the patience of an angel.

The labor before Hanzu's delivery had been long. All night long. But Takash had never lost his poise. The same could not be said of her. The midwife had earned her keep that night. But the delivery had gone well. She remembered what a feeling that had been after it was all over, and little Hanzu nestled at her breast. That was a feeling like no other in the world. She knew she would love this child with all her heart.

Takash had been proud it was a boy - and proud of her, too. They had brought another life into the world together, and it would continue the family name.

Takash had been like a rock for all the emergencies of childhood. Rarely had he lost his temper. Her confidence and trust in him were sometimes overwhelming. But now ... oh, now, the loss was an ever present ache, sometimes muted, other times flaring up like a fire, and always like a hole in her being. The bull had broken its harness and had gored Takash, as he struggled with it. He had fallen and bled to death. She had seen the blood, as the farm hands brought him in - a lifeless corpse by then. She was grateful Hanzu had been away. That would have been unbearable for her had he been there.

She remembered the time down by the stream at night - the night Takash had proposed to her. She knew it was coming. Takash was an earnest, honest man. He was easy for her to read. She smiled. But she loved him. There was never any doubt in her mind. He could not sing; he was not an educated man, but he had heart, and she felt that, always felt that. His manners were plain, but sincere, and conveyed the certainty she would be well taken care of. She remembered how she had smiled at his awkward words; how she had said yes, quietly, and leaned her head on his shoulder. How slowly he had kissed her - and how tenderly he held her.

She tucked Hanzu into bed and moved into her room. A few rivulets of tears washed slowly down her face, as she laid her head on the pillow and sought the sleep that would take away the pain for a few hours.

CHAPTER 6

THE WORKSHOP

Sebastian awoke the next morning and decided to visit Uesugo in his shop on Kobayashi Lane. It was not a long walk from the inn, but he took his time and enjoyed the leisurely stroll through part of the town. Japan was a strange place. How did he ever get here? But the more he saw, the more familiar it became. He arrived at Uesugo's shop about ten o'clock in the morning. As he entered, the smell of wood and varnish wafted into his senses. It was a good smell, suggesting a feeling of home. He greeted one of the workmen at the door and was shown into the workshop area.

"Ah, *Ohayo gozimasu, Koku-jin,*" Uesugo greeted him. "*Hajime mashite?*" He queried, coming towards him to shake his hand.

"Good morning, too. I am fine," he replied. "And you?"

"We are fast at work. Not a moment to lose. But everything is going well. Here, come and see." Uesugo led him around the large workroom. "Over here, we are doing the slides. First the wood strips are cut - there. Not too hard to do. Then the holes are bored over here." He indicated another workman at a different table. "That takes a bit more time, and we have to finish the holes by filing any rough spots smooth. Over there we are gluing the top piece - should be ready tomorrow."

They moved around the room to where leather was being stitched.

"I am not a leather worker," Uesugo went on, but Mikata, here, has had some experience."

"How do you seal the leather to the transfer pipe or the bellows wood?" Sebastian inquired.

"Well, this is difficult," responded Uesugo. "We use a glue, but it is weak. Won't last. So we can tack it, or use a band and tack that - kind of like the bands about a pickle barrel or a saké barrel. Or we can use a screw clamp. This is more difficult, but the seal is better, and you can adjust it, if a leak develops. So that's what we are doing. I think it will work fine."

"And the tracking rods?" he went on.

"Ah, those. We are making progress. I think we have a few done already." Uesugo moved to another of the artisans. "Yoshi, here, is working as fast as he can. The cuts are finer, and the work goes slower. He turned to Sebastian. "Here," he said, picking up a few of the long slender pieces. "This is what we have so far."

He took them in his hands. "Hmmm," he murmured. "These look good." He bent them slightly. "Not too flexible. Not too brittle, either. That is good." He smiled at Uesugo. "You love to work with wood."

"I love everything about it." Uesugo smiled back. "The smell of raw, well-seasoned wood. The way it shapes to your hand under the working of a tool. The variety of characteristics - the maple and the pine, the oak, the walnut, the beech and the birch. The difference in the grain is fascinating. I love the way it looks when it is finished. A glowing patina that suggests ... that ... I don't know how to say it - something comfortable, something human, that you can touch and feel its natural beauty." He shook his head. "I don't know what else I would do. I am not a farmer, or a banker, or a teacher. But wood - furniture - is my life. I do love it."

He observed the busy, but careful goings on in the workshop. It seemed more than Uesugo loved his work here.

"Why don't we move to my office and look at some of the sketches we have made for the wind chest?" Uesugo indicated a room near the back.

On the way, they passed an old man sitting on a platform in the corner, whittling away at a small stump of wood. He looked almost one hundred years of age, mostly bald with only few, short gray hairs showing around the back of his head. His skin was tanned but wrinkled, and his concentration on his task was total. Using a single sharp knife that looked like a butcher's cleaver, he went about his work carefully and deliberately, as if doing it as a ritual. There were small pots of black and gold ink nearby, and the completed works were off to the right a bit. They were likenesses of a bird, with sharply cut features. But the feathers had been made to curl and flex by the way they had been cut - like wood shavings, curling, but not quite cut off entirely. It was a most artistic creation. The bird's features were made visible by hand painting them from the inkpots. The eyes were fierce looking, and the talons appeared to grip the base with intense, savage strength.

"Is that an eagle?" He asked.

Uesugo halted. "No, that is a hawk - the hawk of Yonezawa. My grandfather makes them here. It is his work - and, at this age, his life." He moved over to the palette, bowed slightly to the man working there, who nodded barely perceptibly. He picked up a small, finished sample.

"Here, *Koku-jin*. Take it. It is yours. It will be something to remember us by."

Sebastian took the carved wooden figure in his hand, turning it over and examining the workmanship and the artistry and put it in his satchel.

"It looks like you are making good progress," he said, getting back to the business at hand, as he sat down opposite Uesugo at a desk in the office.

"Yes, it is going well - better than I thought possible. We had the wood on hand, and it was well seasoned, so we don't have to worry so much about it changing shape after it is cut," responded Uesugo. "But we are careful to clamp everything, nonetheless."

"Do you think Matsui-san will be a problem in this?" he queried his helper with a sidelong glance.

"There's no telling what he will do," replied Uesugo. "He does not seem to be a bad person at heart, but he is very intense, and he may do anything to get Hana-ko's attention."

"Ah," he mused aloud. "And how do you feel about that?"

Uesugo took a deep breath. "I suppose, one could say, we are rivals."

"And who has the upper hand?"

"After the delays we have had in the past, I think no one. Hana-ko is very stubborn and not in the mood for returning affection or responding to ... to interest."

"So, you are not the favorite."

"No. But neither is Matsui-san. Hana-ko is just not ready to move on with her life. She is bitter - not extravagantly or outwardly, but she has withdrawn - just not interested - in anything - singing, men, whatever. Only Hanzu is her precious possession now. She is still quite devoted to him."

"He is a fine lad. I can see why. And you hope to change this situation?"

"Yes, but it will take time. I did not know Takash very well. He was a farmer, not a tradesman. But their relationship was close. When she lost him, she blamed God. We could all see the change. She was a wonderful singer. Beautiful, uplifting, inspiring. Now, we have neither her nor the organ. I think the whole town feels it. I certainly do."

"Hmmm," he responded thoughtfully. "It is never good to have bad things multiply. I will do my best to do what I can, but it is always God who gives the grace." He rose from his seat and extended his hand. "Together - soon we have success. I will take another look at the console and see what I can do there. Your work here is very encouraging, Uesugo. Without the horse, one cannot win the race."

CHAPTER 7

PRESSURE TEST

Three days later, the artisans were grumbling around the console in the church. Pleased, Uesugo was with them.

"Three days," said the first artisan. "Unbelievable. I never thought it could be done.

"Well, we did manage to do this," replied the second, "but we are not completely done. The ranks above are next."

"I don't think they're quite as bad," replied the first.

"Well, we have made a lot more progress than Matsui-san has with Hana-ko, eh?" A third joked.

Some laughed, but one of them said, "Not to fool with that. Matsui-san is a serious man. Not in a mood to be made a laughingstock at this point, I think. If we succeed, if *Koku-jin* succeeds, how do you think that will make him feel? He is the dispenser of medicine for this town. Maybe we should not be so hard on him."

Uesugo was about to enter the conversation, when Bach and Hanzu entered the church and moved towards the men.

"Well, gentlemen, everything in order?" Bach queried. "Everything done?"

There were nods of assent from the artisans and mumblings of "Yes, sir."

"Well, not exactly *everything*, *Koku-jin*," responded Uesugo. "But we have installed quite a bit. It seems tight."

"Shall we try it, then?" Bach asked.

The artisans looked at each other.

"What? Already?" The second artisan asked incredulously. "But, *Koku-jin*, we are not finished, no? The pipes? The tracking rods?"

"We will get there," replied Bach. "But first to find out whether the wind holds up. The wind is the heart of the machine. No wind, ... no power, no sound, ... no nothing. Without the wind, the organ is silent. If we cannot get the wind, there is no use moving on."

Bach sent Uesugo and another of the artisans to the pedal room.

"Pressure up," he shouted.

They started at the bellows and step cranks. The bellows moved slowly with a quiet swooshing sound, and the air pressure in the wind chest began to build. Uesugo went to look at the water gauge to measure the pressure. The level of water in the tube began to rise.

"Two inches," he yelled to Bach below, "three inches of pressure."

The other artisans quickly ran to check the bellows and the main wind chest.

"No leaks?" Bach's voice rang from the console. "Take it up to four inches! Hold pressure. Stop pedaling."

They did as Bach commanded and stopped.

"Check pressure," Bach's voice rang out again.

"It's holding," the artisan replied excitedly. "Very steady." He waited a few seconds, as Uesugo went over to verify the reading.

"Very slightly moving down," Uesugo added. "But only a little. Hardly to be seen. It's working."

"Very good," Bach shouted, then added softly, "now for the console."

Uesugo poked his head out of the wind chest door and observed Bach approaching the keyboard. Bach looked at the keys for a minute, then laid his arms across as many as possible. A sudden roar rang from the pipes, as the wind pressure did its job to make the sound.

Uesugo held his ears as the noise, a huge, disharmonious cacophony, rang through the church.

The noise jolted a monk quietly pursuing his job of copying the Scripture in the deeper recesses of the church. A second loud noise jolted him again, causing him to drop his pen on the page where an inkblot resulted.

"Dammit," he exclaimed, outraged. He threw down the pen in exasperation. "What in thunderation was that?"

It would be just that moment when the rector appeared in the doorway.

"Yoshi-ban!" the rector chided.

The monk looked up, blushed somewhat and replied sheepishly, "ah, forgive me, Rector, but what is going on here to disturb my peace? That was louder than a thunderclap. Scared me half to death. My copying is ruined."

"It's that *Koku-jin* - come to fix the organ. Let's go see."

Sebastian was about to try the third rank by laying his arm across the keyboard with his "everything" technique, as the rector and a most disgruntled monk arrived at the console. The rector was tall and moved with the assurance of practiced authority. The monk was dark haired, on the portly side and noticeably shorter.

"What kind of sound are you making?" the monk demanded. "The organ should play music - not thunder. Heavenly harmonies - not noise. You disturb the peace of this holy place with that infernal racket. Can't you ... can't you ...?"

The monk was left gasping for words, as Sebastian turned slowly. He was about to launch into a testy riposte, but took a deep breath as he caught sight of Rector Uetake.

"Ahhhh ... I am sorry, dear sir," he replied carefully and apologetically with a slight bow, "for disturbing your peace. Perhaps you should have been notified beforehand. My fault." He bowed in a conciliatory gesture. "Please forgive me. But we are fixing the organ, and we need to do this. We need to find out what is working and what isn't. We cannot wait. Later, the sound will please both you and me much more."

"Well ..." The monk seemed to accept the explanation, but did not look entirely pleased. "I will return when you are finished," he said quietly.

"We will be all day today, probably a few more days after that," Sebastian replied.

"What? With all this noise?" the monk shot back, giving the rector a quick glance.

The rector shrugged, and the monk sighed and walked away briskly.

Sebastian elbowed the third rank of keys. A loud higher-pitched sound resulted, startling the poor monk again, who jerked, but continued on his way out of the sanctuary.

"Well, *Koku-jin*" The rector was in an ebullient mood. "That's the first sound we've heard from this instrument in almost two years," he said enthusiastically. "It looks like things are going well, eh?" He followed up his comments with a look that seemed to expect a progress report.

"The workers have done their job well, Rector," he replied in a businesslike manner, though he, too, was pleased. "But now it is I who must do his job well."

He looked at Rector Uetake quietly, expecting him to move on, but it seemed the rector anticipated more, as he eyed Sebastian as if still looking for some explanation. But none was forthcoming.

"Well, then, carry on," the rector said cheerfully, turned and walked out.

Sebastian watched the man quietly, and then he turned back to the workers. "Gentlemen, you have done well. Now we need to do the rest. When the batch of slide stops is done at the shop, bring them here right away. We'll fit them directly. There will be beer and *sushi* for you all at the tavern. Good lunch."

Ahhh, that was something they could all warm up to. There was lots of positive muttering, as they congregated to leave.

"It's about time we got a break," muttered one.

"After this morning, this will be the best lunch we've had in awhile," replied another.

"I hope the others take their time, eh?" A third joked.

"But I will need you and you." Sebastian pointed to two of the artisans, who groaned, "for the bellows and the power. Somebody come back and help them in an hour."

As they all left, he turned to Hanzu, who had been sitting in the pew.

"Now, Hanzu, we need to tune," he said matter of factly.

The boy jumped up eagerly and followed him to one of the ranks.

CHAPTER 8

TUNING

Hanzu looked up at the organ pipes, row upon row, all clean and set in their ranks. There were six hundred and sixty of them. Small pipes, medium pipes, pipes with reeds to make sounds like a wind instrument of the *haut bois* type. Pipes to give sounds like the trumpet, and pipes cut to give sound based on the whistle principle - like the *Blockflöte*. There were big pipes, larger than he was, larger than *Koku-jin,* a few of them sixteen feet tall. Those went almost to the top of the church. They would have to build a special scaffold to tune them. He looked in silence for a minute, sensing the majesty of the place and the expectation of music to come. It just wasn't there, yet, but he could feel something in his bones. Something magnificent was about to happen, and he was going to be a part of it. The wonder of it all froze him in his steps, when Bach's voice gradually broke into his reverie.

"Now like this for the main pipes," said Bach showing him how to coil or uncoil a metal strip cut parallel to the pipe axis. "Out, in, so. I will tell you when to stop. For the reeds it is the same, except you move this rod to shorten or lengthen the vibration distance. You have to be a little more careful here. And for the wooden pipes, we tap the stop with a small hammer - gently, or pull up the stop - also gently. The movements are not likely to be large, so you do have to be careful. Just tap a little, all right?" Bach showed him a small reed pipe.

The thin metal sheet comprising the reed was delicate, and the thin metal tuning rod was about the thickness of a finishing nail. One end was bent back on itself into a "T" shape to put even pressure on the reed, and the other was bent into a circle, so it could be grasped and moved more easily.

"But the same thing," Bach went on, "out, in. I'll tell you when to stop. All right?"

He nodded. When Bach returned to the console, he remained among the ranks.

"Wind up!" Bach shouted to the two artisans. "About three inches of pressure - not too high, just keep it thereabouts."

After a confirming yell from the chest room, Bach pressed a key; and the note sounded. "Too flat!" he yelled. "Roll the strip down a bit." He pressed the key again. "Too much, back out just a little." Once more he pressed the key. "There, that's it. Good!"

He pressed the next key an octave above. The same. Again. Octaves and unisons first, starting at middle C. All up and down the range of the organ. Hanzu had to hustle to find all the pipes. The fifths were next, then the fourths. This was a little more difficult. Bach ordered him to find the perfect interval first, then to very delicately adjust the pipe to his attentive ear listening for the beat pattern of just slightly out-of-tune notes. In this way the equal-tempered scale was set. The thirds and sixths were next, the same way.

On and on it went. The next key, the next job, one after the other. Key after key. Minute after minute. Hour after hour. It seemed forever before they stopped for lunch.

Lunch was a generous meal of raw fish, rice and green leafy salad. To drink, there was beer and a little saké for the adults, while he had to settle for some green tea. They ate slowly, savoring every morsel.

"Not an easy job, eh?" Bach said, looking over at him.

"I *am* tired. There sure are a lot of pipes," he said, breathing out a big sigh. "But it was fun. I can't imagine anyone tuning this whole thing out of his head!"

"Well," Bach smiled, "we did two ranks complete, plus a little more. You look like you need rest. Time to play some music. Are you ready?"

"I'm too tired - even to try. But I'd love to watch you," he replied. "How do you play music with nothing to read from?"

"It's all very simple, really," Bach smiled again. "When you know how. Just one note after the other." He thought a moment. "Here, we'll start with these - like this - do ... me ... re..." He held a little longer on the "re" than the others, like one, twoooo, threeeeeee. "Now, what do you make of that?"

"I don't know," he replied, mystified. "It doesn't sound like music. Just three notes. What is so interesting about that?"

"Well, you are right," Bach said, his hands moving above the keys a little. "It needs something more. It needs to be a theme, a tune, something you can hold in your head, whistle or hum a bit." He paused. "How about this?" He continued the notes, "do ti re do ti fa si do. Not enough, not enough. Needs more," mused Bach. He hesitated a bit. "How about this?" Warming up to his task, he began to play the *Fugue in G minor* in earnest.

"And this," he continued. "Now all together - with a little harmony." He played the bars through.

"Wow. It seemed so simple at first, then ..." Hanzu looked on in amazement. "Oh my, how did you do that?"

Bach smiled. "Just one note after the other," he said plainly.

"But is that all there is to it?" He quizzed in disbelief.

"Oh, no," Bach replied. "This is where only the musician can go. Let me explain it this way. Music must start somewhere - like the first three notes. It must have some kind of theme - like we did before." His hands were moving on the keys again. "But then it must go somewhere - and that can be almost anywhere. Here is one way." He continued with a counter melody. "Then you can bring back the theme - but not the same way - otherwise you might bore people - and musicians cannot bore people. It is the worst sin. You will lose people's interest that way, and music is about the opposite - about inspiring people." He continued playing, more softly now.

The keys sang under his tutelage. It seemed effortless, ... and magnificent. Hanzu had never heard anything quite like it.

"You can develop the theme for a while," Bach went on, "maybe use several themes at once. But then you must bring it to an end - a conclusion - to leave people with closure, with satisfaction - with a good feeling." He continued towards the ending. "This is what gives them hope and courage for the future."

"But what about all those notes?" he asked. "Most instruments only play one note at a time, but the organ plays so many at once."

"Only so many as you have fingers." Bach laughed.

"But an organist can use his feet, too - no? How can you do all of that?" he inquired.

Bach thought for a minute. "You are talking about the harmony part of music," he responded. "That is the soul. This is very complicated for a young man like you. You have to train for this - like an apprentice or journeyman. But maybe it would sound like this." He played the selection through again, a little fuller this time. "And you have to have a rhythm - a regular beat to keep the music going." He indicated such with note emphasis on the keyboard. "Otherwise the music lags," he went on. "When you have no pulse, you are dead. It is the same with the rhythm. And then - to put it all together - that is what I do - make music."

"It's so wonderful," he said in appreciation, Abut can you live on this? Do so many people like this? Do they feel as I do?"

"The court, the church - yes, they pay me," replied Bach. "It is not very much, so I also teach. Most professional musicians must do something like that to have enough to support a wife and family - with kids - like you." He smiled. "Well, tomorrow I think we have more work to do, but it can wait till then. Now we can go home."

CHAPTER 9

THE INN OF HAPPINESS

Well, Hanzu, you look quite tired," said Hana-ko as she greeted Sebastian and her son at the door of the inn. "Must have been a tough day for a young boy. What did you do?"

Hanzu shuffled through the door with a tired gait; as if he wanted nothing more than to plop on the ground right there and go to sleep. He had never looked so tired.

"Oh, Mother," he replied, "it was so much. I did so much work. I couldn't even tell you half." Then looking at Bach, he went on. "But the music ..."

"Really?" She looked a little quizzically at Sebastian, then back to Hanzu. "You got the organ to work already?"

"Oh, Mother, you should have been there," Hanzu said tiredly, stifling a big yawn. "But I am really tired. May I go to bed?" he asked plaintively, looking at her with big doe eyes that he could hardly keep open.

"Yes, my dear, my darling boy." She kissed him affectionately. "You will be a man someday. But tonight - sleep well."

"Tomorrow we might finish," said Hanzu with a sudden, but short-lived, burst of energy. He turned and went slowly up the stairs.

She followed him with her eyes. He was such a precious child. It was wonderful to be a mother, even if she was lonely. She turned back to Sebastian.

"So, you made music today? That hasn't happened here for over two years. You actually got it to work?"

"Yes," he replied. "Hanzu was a great help. He was a willing worker - a fine lad."

"Thank you," she replied. "It's nice to hear such praise about one's child." She turned to the clavichord. "Could you play something for me, *Koku-jin?*"

"Well ..." Sebastian hesitated a bit. "I do have some music with me, if you are willing to sing a little - quietly, maybe." He looked at her while he took out some sheets from his bag and went slowly to the clavichord.

As he sat down and placed the music on the ledger, she came over to take a quick look, curious as to what she would find. He started to play *Dir, Dir...*

He nodded to her for the voice part. She tried, singing the *dirs* of the first stanza. She got through the first two lines, but then she stopped. Sebastian went on for a few bars then stopped, too, and looked at her.

"You don't like it?" he asked.

"Oh, no. It's lovely," she said. "I didn't expect that. I ..."

"It is a song of praise to God," he explained. "Sometimes we need a reminder."

"It's not that at all," she replied softly. "It was wonderful. I never heard such beautiful music."

"Well then," he went on, "could we continue?"

"Uhhh, no, ... not now." She took a deep breath, her emotions racing and confused. "Please. I am really not ... ready."

"Music that is part of one's life, one never forgets," he replied softly.

"I should follow Hanzu to bed," she said, drying her tears with her handkerchief.

Sebastian slowly placed the sheets of music back in his bag. "Sometimes it helps to talk," he said to her quietly.

"All right," she said after a small hesitation. She tried to quiet herself.

They both moved back to the table and sat down facing each other.

"Something to drink?" Sebastian inquired, as the serving girl came over.

"Yes. Some *saké*," she replied quietly.

"Two," he said to the servant, as she left to get the drinks.

"What is that?" he asked a little on guard.

"It is Japanese rice wine - made a little bit more like beer, but without the carbonation, and lots more alcohol, like wine."

"Does it taste like that wasabi?"

"No. It is very mild, subtle. The one they have here is made in town. It is very nice. Has a fruity component ... like pears, but not sweet. I don't know what to compare it to. You have to try it and see."

The table servant returned with the drinks, and Sebastian took a sip.

"Almost like white wine," he said. "Not so tangy, but stronger. Back home I love a good Riesling - like *Ockfener Bockstein* - with a little, tart kick that livens up a good meal."

The interlude helped quiet her somewhat. Bach placed his hand on hers and looked into her eyes.

"Sometimes not saying anything is best for a wounded heart," he said softly. "Other times, talking is better."

"It's hard to know what is best at all anymore." She spoke with a mixture of frustration, pain and confusion.

"You are getting some attention from Matsui-san? And Uesugo?" he quizzed her carefully.

"How did you know?" she said, suddenly on guard.

"Let's not worry about that now," he replied. "More than one person thinks it's time you moved on with your life."

"Matsui-san was not very kind to you," she said.

"Yes, I know," he replied. "It did disturb me a little, but there are many difficult people in this world. I've had my share to deal with. It hasn't been easy for me. Matsui-san is not in a very good position. I can understand why he is opposed to me." He removed his hand from hers. "Do you love him?" He asked quietly.

"No," she said immediately. "I am aware of his intentions, but I am not in love with him. I am not ready for any man, even Uesugo - I may never be. Takash was such a good man. You couldn't understand. I don't want another."

"You may be right. But, Hanzu needs a father, don't you think? You may not be ready - for a lot of things. I say this gently, please," he hastened to add. "There will come a time when you will be. I know this. You can move on - when you are ready. It does take time. Your feelings will never disappear, if you loved truly. But something else will happen. You will grow beyond them. Your husband will always be a part of your life, but your life will be different - larger. There will be other parts of that life that will become more important, more immediate - no disrespect to your husband. But he is dead, and you are alive. Here. In this world. You must live in it - not in some world you cannot attain."

She did not know what to make of this foreigner standing before her. Something in her agreed with his eminent common sense, and something else found it impossible to agree. And there was Matsui-san. He was a respected man in the community - a dispenser of medicine. That was important and attractive. He had been a help to many - and he had tried hard to fix the organ. It just wasn't him. But nobody else had been able to either, until *Koku-jin* came along. Underneath, she knew he spoke from experience. This was not just a talk to make her feel better. There was something of life in *Koku-jin* - some quality that rang true to life - in the midst of its pain and sorrow. But she did not know what to make of it. The complexity was too much for her.

"Thank you," she said quietly. "Now, I really must be going to bed." She rose slowly and murmured another "thank you" and walked up the stairs uncertain just how she should feel.

CHAPTER 10

HAIKU

On the next evening, Sebastian paid a visit to Uesugo at his home in response to an invitation. Doffing his shoes just inside the door, as was the custom, he was received into the living room of Uesugo's small, but tidy house. On the mantelpiece of the fireplace were many copies of the hawk of Yonezawa.

"Konbanwa, Koku-jin," greeted Uesugo.

"Yes, good evening," he responded in turn. "I see your grandfather has been quite active ... and productive." He indicated the mantelpiece.

"Yes, it is a wonderful thing for the aged to feel useful, and indeed to be useful. That way they are not forgotten. It is an old custom here. Of course, my grandfather was a wood-worker, too. But his specialty was carving; mine is building."

"How is it that a Christian church got to be here, in Japan?" He asked.

"Dutch protestant missionaries, about two hundred years ago - in the south," replied Uesugo thoughtfully. "The Portuguese were first. The Catholic Church was first here.

They were free to see all of Japan for a few years. Then the Shogunate confined them to an island in the south - for trading purposes, and so they could be carefully watched. But several of the churches in other parts of Japan persisted. We are far away from the center of Japan, and whatever foreigners come here are too few for the regime to worry about. Korea, China, Russia are all just across the sea of Japan. Very close really. Easy to go back and forth.

"And the hawk?" He inquired.

"Ahh. It is an ancient myth of Japan. This is the mountain country - Yonezawa, where the hawks live. *Nihon-ji* is a mythical city-state of the Japanese people. The hawk is always circling above - gazing down, always waiting to defeat evil on the part of the good. Ready to fall with fierce strength on those who do wickedness on others. It is a two-edged sword. The evil can be without ... or within."

"Ah," he said, "a kind of guardian angel."

"Yes. A protector."

"Are there legends written about it?"

"There is a *Haiku*," replied Uesugo moving over to pick up a scroll from a table in the corner of the room. "Here, I'll read it to you. A Haiku is a Japanese-style poem. The strophes are of seventeen syllables usually arranged five-seven-five, unrhyming. It goes like this."

He began to read from the scroll.

THE HAWK OF YONEZAWA

My creator - man
Of eighty - long at his bench -
Well versed. On a post

I perch, wait to soar -
My wings and talons outlined
In ink - black and gold.

My feathers springy
Shavings of wood, cut by the
Artful Master's blade,

All from a single staff.
I soar and seek the highest
And fear no one.

My eyes ever wake:
My gaze fixed on those below,
Lest evil befall.

"And this is the legend my grandfather keeps alive."

"It is a lovely sentiment. I am sure it would be a popular one, too," Sebastian added.

"I agree. That is why I asked you over tonight. I have another guest coming that I thought you would like to meet. A *Gaijin* - a foreigner like you. He is a shopkeeper from Russia - Vladivostok - not too far away, actually. We sell him the hawks and other handmade sundries - lamps, pottery, dyed silk, items like that. It is a good business."

There was a knocking at the door, and the Russian entered. He was a bear of a man with a huge beard and a large, dark-colored cloak.

"*Konbanwa,* Uesugo. *Hajime mashite,*" he boomed with a deep and hearty voice. "Ah, who is this?" He asked, taking off his shoes and moving into the living room.

"Ah, this is our *Koku-jin* - a German. He is a musician - here to fix the organ of the church."

"Well, that will be something. Hello," the Russian said, offering his hand to Sebastian. "I am Sergei. I am here to see *aka-baku.*" He smiled, rubbing his hands together with anticipation.

"What is *aka-baku?*" Sebastian whispered to Uesugo.

"Ah, yes," replied Uesugo first to the Russian. "Please sit down and have some tea." Then to Sebastian he motioned to sit also and replied to them both. "Aka-baku is a hand painted, *papier-maché* model of a cow. She has a bobbing head. Children love her. It was the custom many years ago for all guests in Japan to paint *aka-baku.* The base coat, painted red, is already on - the guest uses white to paint the date and whatever designs suit his or her fancy on top of the red. It is the symbol of good fortune and hospitality in Japan. Red and white are the colors of Japan.

"My customers love *aka-baku,*" beamed the Russian. "I can sell it all over the world with the shipping that comes through Vladivostok. For me it is good luck, too." He laughed heartily. "But I am here for the shipment of the hawks, too. Those also do a good business." He eyed the hawks on the mantelpiece. Then he addressed Uesugo. "Ah, maybe fifty of the small-to-medium size, number nine, I think. And twenty of the large ones, number fifteen, I think. That is a little more than last time. They are selling well. Same price as before, I imagine?"

"Yes, of course," said Uesugo. "We will box them and have them ready for you tomorrow morning, about ten o'clock."

"Excellent," exclaimed the Russian, rising and quaffing his tea in a single gulp. "I am out and about tonight. Tomorrow I will stop by the shop. *Oyasumi nasai*" he bowed to them both and left forthwith.

"Yes, good night, too," responded Uesugo.

"Where is he going?" Sebastian queried.

"To the *saké* house. He'll be sampling and buying lots of *saké* there, too. Most of what I do here is local, but international business is most fascinating."

Sebastian spent the rest of the evening in quiet conversation with Uesugo, learning about the customs of Japan and talking of the job ahead. But in his heart he pondered, would he able to finish in time and go home?

CHAPTER 11

FIRST RUN

In the morning, Sebastian was at the church keeping a keen eye on the artisans, who were busily fitting new stop slides to the pipe chests in the upper ranks. The soft muted sound of pegs being hammered, of small saws and files cutting through wood for a final fit, filled the sanctuary. Uesugo was supervising above, while he and Hanzu watched from below.

The first artisan came to the edge of the balcony where they were working, looked over and announced, "Just about finished, *Koku-jin*. We need some time for everything to dry, and you can test it - maybe this afternoon. The slides are moving well, and the seals seem to be holding well."

"I will need pedalers for this afternoon," he said, nodding with approval.

Two of the workmen volunteered. Then Sebastian turned and walked out of the church with Hanzu.

It was about mid-afternoon when they returned to the quiet church. He gazed upwards at the rows of pipes, as they moved down the main aisle. There was an air of something having been finished - and ready.

They went to the console, now fixed and looking almost new. He ran his hands over the wood in an absent-minded, yet affectionate manner. His eyes ran over all the details - the keys, the tracking rods, the stops, the music stand, the bench, and the foot pedals. Then they moved slowly into the main wind chest, observing the repairs. The chest was sound, the bellows leather in excellent shape, the pedal cranks fixed, cleaned and set, the wind pipes leading to the ranks above repaired cleanly. Uesugo had done well.

"Better than I expected. Let's go up, eh?" He said to Hanzu.

They moved up the stairs to the ranks above and looked carefully at what the workmen had done. Everything was set in rows, neatly and carefully placed. Not a speck of dust, the metal parts cleaned and glowing with that dull pewter look that spoke of quiet elegance; the old wood freshly oiled and giving a rich patina impression. It looked like fine furniture. Sebastian felt a bit like a German general on inspection of troops. He could hardly wait to hear how it sounded.

"A little more tuning, Hanzu - the reed pipes. Then we are done." He looked at the boy.

"I'm ready," Hanzu smiled.

Sebastian made his way down to the console, as Hanzu remained above.

"All right," he said, "start with the low A in the reeds." He pulled out a few stops and pressed the key. It was off. "Push in a little on the control rod," he shouted to Hanzu.

"Ready," he said.

Bach pressed the key again. It was on. Hanzu was getting better. He was thrilled and moved to the octave enthusiastically. Once the A's were done, he moved on.

"E," he shouted. "First rank again. Same thing."

Hanzu moved to the "E" pipe and adjusted it in slightly. Bach pressed the key.

"A little more in," he shouted.

And on it went. All morning. Another tedious job. But Hanzu was becoming quite skilled, now. They were almost finished. Was it the expectation of hearing the whole organ come alive that made him excited?

Finally, Sebastian rested from the console.

"All right, Hanzu. Come on down," he said. "it's time for lunch. You have done the job of a man today."

A tired but grinning Hanzu made his way down from the loft. He patted the boy on the shoulders as he came up to the console.

"We done?" Hanzu asked tiredly, but with sparkling eyes.

"Just about," he replied. "Time for some rest for you, though. Why don't you go on home? I need to do just a little more here before my dinner tonight."

Hanzu looked up into his face. I really am tired, but I had so much fun." He took a deep breath, turned and went slowly out of the church. Then he stopped at the door, turned around and waved, a tired smile on his face.

Sebastian smiled to himself, as the small figure disappeared out the door. He shook his head. Children. Hanzu reminded him of his little Carl when he had been that age. Then he turned quietly to the console and started fiddling with the stops, checking the trackers and the keys.

"Wind," he shouted to the pedalers.

They started. Slowly, the water gauge level rose, as the bellows gave their quiet swooshing sound.

"Three inches," yelled one of the pedalers.

"Hold there," he called back. Then he bowed his head at the keyboard, took a big breath and started playing.

Slowly, then more rapidly he ran his fingers up and down the keys, pulling stops to control the registers, moving his feet on the foot pedals in a kind of warm-up. He was playing the Toccata from the *Toccata, Adagio and Fugue in C major*. He could sense the brilliance of the sound and the vibrations of the low notes when he hit them with the foot board. It had good volume, and he hit a few of the deep notes, holding them a little longer for the testing.

Over at the tavern, the artisans could hear.

"What is that?" One of the artisans shouted, his head snapping up from a pint of beer. "Is the earth shaking? Another earthquake?" Earthquakes were common in Japan.

"No, it's the organ. The organ is playing," shouted a second. "Quick. Outside."

They all ran outside. Others came too, from left and right - butcher, baker, tradesmen, and people in the street. Matsui-san and his friends came out of the Apothecary's shop. There was a general buzz of excitement. They could all hear it. "It's the organ. It's fixed."

There was a press toward the church. The rector appeared, looking up at the commotion, and was swept along.

"Go get Hana-ko," someone cried. The crowd arrived at the door, already occupied by Sakura, a blind woman with a very acute sense of hearing. She wore a beatific look on her face, a look that halted the rector in his tracks, as the scene struck him. Some of the crowd pushed through the doors into the sanctuary. The hubbub subsided quickly, as the crowd was awed by what they heard and saw.

Bach was at console playing, the wonderful sounds reverberating from wall to wall in the church, as it never had before. Great C major chords at triple *forte* thundered off the walls. Did it sound so heavenly because they had been without for so long? Or was it this man, this unknown man - come to fix the organ? Or was it something beyond them all?

He ended the piece with a rousing finale - his unperceived audience too stunned to respond. He then took a deep breath and began again with another test for the instrument.

The big, low-note pipes sounded slowly, quietly at first, but the vibrations could be felt. The sounds of the *Passacaglia in C minor* came on deliberately, single notes sounding quietly, paced slowly with deep sonority penetrating through to the listeners' hearts, as if each pipe were speaking directly to them. An air of mystery and awe filled the sanctuary. Slowly the complex melody became clear - totally commanding attention in a deliberate, haunting, measured, arresting way. Then repeated, but differently. The richness of the harmony was shimmeringly complex, full, strangely satisfying and perfect - the persistent, intense tones getting louder and building. They could feel their spines tingling, their hearts being spoken to by the deep, haunting notes of the music, drawing them carefully, slowly, deliberately, inexorably into another world. Bach then shifted a few stops and played the ending.

Then the sound doubled, tripled, quadrupled in intensity. Now the entire town could hear. The crowd became engulfed in a whole world of sound and a world of wonder.

Out in the fields near the town, heads rose, the workers getting a taste of what the crowd inside the church was being immersed in. Sound. Glorious, harmonious, haunting, powerful - almost overpowering - and carrying into the fields even. Was this the voice of God? One by one, the workers slowly put down their tools and joined others on their way to the church, all the while the music calling them. Persistent, powerful, authoritative, irresistible. A second wave of people approached the church in awe, some slowly filing in behind others.

Sakura remained at the door, her ear pressed to the oak, her eyes closed and the broadest smile of satisfaction on her face.

Hana-ko pushed her way through the crowd, eventually viewing Sebastian at the console, oblivious to it all. She was stunned by the music and the majesty. She slumped into a pew, almost overcome, the incredulity of the experience running through her soul.

He finished the rousing finale at triple *forte* on the console, holding the note over for effect and finality.

Then he took another deep breath and plunged into yet another test of the organ. This was the Fugue of the *Toccata, Adagio and Fugue in C major*. A sudden and loud shift back to a major tonality from the minor struck the listeners. The rhythmic, tuneful theme bounded from wall to wall. It was as if the pipes had started to dance. The sounds filled not only the church, but the listeners' hearts as well. He noticed a little reverb after the first few bars and responded by giving the unfolding of the music a little wait, here and there, to emphasize the effect. Hana-ko felt herself rising in the pew. Was it her body? Or her soul? Her heart warming as never before in response to music so uplifting, it seemed to be spoken by the voice of God Himself.

There it was, finally, a rousing end. She was stunned along with all the others at what they had just witnessed. There was no response. There couldn't be. Clapping seemed so inappropriate. Cheering was something one did at sports events or the theater. Only silence seemed sufficient. Completely awed silence.

That was it - a moment of holy quiet that seemed to hang in the air - until the rector took charge. He approached from the back of the church, clapping loudly, if awkwardly. Someone had to, and it did break the mood.

"My God, *Koku-jin*." The rector looked a bit sheepish and apologetic. "Magnificent. We did not know. What a splendid job you did. And the organ. I never heard it sound better. Incredible."

Sebastian moved off the console seat and bowed politely.

"You must see me on the morrow," said the rector. "We must talk."

CHAPTER 12

THE OBSERVER

It was the next day, and Matsui-san had heard - the music, the buzz of the crowd, the comments. This *Koku-jin* was not the man he had first supposed. Now he seemed super human, but that created even more problems. He had passed by the inn and glanced through the window the night *Koku-jin* and Hana-ko had been talking at the table. He had seen *Koku-jin*'s hand on hers, and she crying softly. And now with *Koku-jin*'s talent made manifest, he felt himself and his cause for Hana-ko's hand lost beyond redemption. What could he do?

Thoughts raced through his head. Not a single good one. No options made sense. He had tried his best and failed. But he wanted Hana-ko more than anything. In his desperation, anger began to arise. The intensifying grip of his tortured emotions would not let him go. His rival had won - for now. He needed to make a response.

His thoughts went briefly back to Sapporo, where his suit for the mayor's daughter, Izumi, had been rejected. She was beautiful - all he had ever dreamed of in a woman. Apothecary was not the trade desired by her family, and he had lost out to a magistrate of the law. She had been won over by his rival's commanding presence and his way with words. Matsui-san was called a technician - a tradesman - by the family. It seemed to her, too. And so he had lost the love he wanted. He had never spoken of that in town, except to his closest friends. He did not want that to happen again, but here it was. And the pain was back, too.

He tried to reason with himself. Yes, it did look bad, and he felt awful. But life here was decent, really. He had a measure of respect. He did good work for those in need and earned a good living from it. There was little competition. But he had failed to fix the organ. And he may have failed with Hana-ko. Who was this *Koku-jin*? Where did he come from? Surely he would not stay. He was not Japanese. He would be moving on. Maybe *Koku-jin* was even married. If he were patient, time would give him another chance. But could he wait? And how long?

Then there was Uesugo. He suspected the woodworker was also interested in Hana-ko. And he was riding *Koku-jin*'s coattails directly into Hana-ko's heart. He gnashed his teeth at the thought and the unfairness of it all. Something dramatic was what he needed to reverse his fortunes. Something bold, but what?

The apothecary's shop was quiet that day. That was a little unusual. There were always customers, those that needed bandages, medicine or herbal cures of some kind or another. Life in the town may have been routine, but there was always something happening. So he retired to the back room - the preparation room. Shelves and shelves of herbal extracts and powders of various colors in bottles were lined up on the shelves; liquids of various kinds arranged the same on the opposite wall. Stores of vinegar, *saké*, spirit. It was a well-ordered place, and for him, comforting. He had apprenticed a long time in Sapporo before coming here. He knew his medicines like the back of his hand. There wasn't too much that escaped him. The window of the room looked out on a back garden where he grew herbs. He turned to the bench on the sidewall of the room and started mixing another vial. This was a potion for Madam Ito - for headaches. He carefully poured the mixture into a bottle and stopped it with a cork, when the door to the shop opened. He put down the bottle, turned and moved into the anteroom to greet the customer.

"Hana-ko!" he said almost in shock. "What brings you here?"

"I am here to pick up Madam Ito's medicine. She cannot come today. Do you have it ready?"

"Yes. Just finished. Wait a bit." He went to the back room and fetched the bottle. Returning, he said, "Here it is - five hundred yen."

Hana-ko fished in her bag for the money.

"So, he fixed the organ," he said plainly.

"Yes," she replied calmly. "It was wonderful. The rector has plans for something. He's speaking to *Koku-jin* tomorrow."

"Really," he said, trying to sound disinterested.

"Yes. He probably wants him to do something special for the church."

"Will you be singing?" He asked.

Hana-ko looked down. "I don't think so. I haven't volunteered. I don't feel ready."

"Hana, I ..."

She cut him off quickly with a sharp glance. "I have no time for talk, Matsui-san. Neither does Madam Ito. She needs this quickly. Thank you for the medicine." She placed the coins for the medicine on the counter and turning sharply, and walked out.

Now his heart pounded. But, now he knew where she stood. If she was not ready for him, she couldn't be ready for anyone else, either, least of all Uesugo ... or *Koku-jin*. That gave him hope. His mind started teeming with ideas. He turned and went into the back room to make up more prescriptions.

Maybe he had been too hard on *Koku-jin*. Maybe *Koku-jin* was not a rival at all. Maybe he would be moving on shortly. Nevertheless, his success contrasted badly with his own failure, and that acid ate at his soul.

The bell to the shop sounded again. He moved into the anteroom in response. Constable Hiddeki and his assistant were coming through the door carefully. The assistant was holding his arm close to his body.

"Little accident," said the constable. "Fujimoto, here, fell while we were chasing horse thieves."

"How did that happen?" he queried.

"We heard some shots over by Kujo's farm. We thought they were hunters out of season. Went over to have a little talk," Hiddeki replied. "When we got there," the constable continued, "we found old Kujo on all fours, having been roughed up a bit."

"Horse thieves, he said," added Fujimoto in a little raspy voice. "He showed us the direction they had taken, and we took out after them."

"Did you get them?" Matsui-san asked.

"No," replied the constable. "We didn't get sight of them, but we tracked them for miles. Then Fujimoto's horse stumbled, and off the saddle he came. Hurt his arm."

"Let's have a look," he said, as he gingerly felt the arm for a possible break. "Hurt here?" he questioned.

"No, not really" was the reply.

"Here?"

"No."

"Make a fist."

Fujimoto did as he was told.

"Hurt?"

"A little."

"Twist your wrist some."

Matsui-san pressed gently near the tendon at the elbow.

"Ohhhh," moaned Fujimoto.

"Bad sprain," he said. "You will need a sling. Come."

They all moved into the back room, where Fujimoto got his arm sling and some herbal potion for the pain.

As they left, he began to muse intently. An idea started to form in his head.

CHAPTER 13

APPOINTMENT

Rector Uetake sat behind his desk in the church office. It was about ten in the morning. The office was a sparse affair, with a few religious paintings on the walls, some small statuary here and there, two of the walls lined with bookshelves and books from credenza-height almost to the ceiling. A set of windows on one side gave it substantial light. Sebastian faced the pastor with his back to the door. There were several others in the room, including Uesugo.

"Well, *Koku-jin,*" the rector began carefully, "you can hardly go so soon. Really, this is a great day for us. And you have done it. We only want to show our appreciation. We simply must have a celebration. It would mean so much to this congregation."

"But rector - no disrespect, but I have been here already two weeks." Bach was more than a little anguished. "The organ is fixed, that's two weeks longer than I should be. My employers will not be pleased. I have a family to support. I cannot risk losing my job."

Rector Uetake waved his hand, as if to dismiss the difficulty with that action. "We will write a note - a special letter explaining our need for you right now. We'll send it by special coach tomorrow." He nodded to Yoshi-ban, who bowed and disappeared out the door.

"Now the piece," the rector went on, "a High Mass, or something like that. An Easter celebration, something big ..." His hands described a large circle as he continued, his eyes enlarged and excited. "... the whole church, towns around. We'll invite everybody! Of course, you will do the music. We didn't know you had such talent. How long will it take you?" He looked at Sebastian intently. "A few days should be enough, no?"

"I hardly ..." He, at a loss for words, could not believe how this was developing. His agitation was becoming more heated by the moment.

"Perhaps you have something suitable with you?" the rector suggested, trying to alleviate Sebastian's obvious discomfort. "Musicians always carry something with them - no? Come, we will pay for your stay. What do you say?"

He hesitated. The last comment brought him up short. It was his duty to serve God with music. How could he turn this down?

"Well, I don't know," he said, looking for a little more time to make a decision. "How long were you thinking?"

"I can't really judge these things." The rector looked around at the others. "What do you all think? A week ... or two?"

The others nodded. Two weeks minimum, they agreed.

"A week?" he exclaimed. "Or two?" Then he responded more resignedly. "Perhaps a week I can do - but it will be very busy. Practice will be intense. I will need everyone's absolute cooperation."

"We will probably need two weeks, absolutely ... maybe three," replied the rector, probing. "Can we have it?"

"I really must be getting back," he said, starting to get piqued. Then he sighed. "If we need it - but no more."

"Well, that settles it." The rector smiled broadly and patted him on the back. "This evening," he spoke to another cleric in the room, "you can call the choir and the singers."

The one spoken to bowed in return.

"We'll have an orchestra ..." the rector said enthusiastically.

CHAPTER 14

THE PLOT

So, how is this again?"

Matsui-san was in the back room of his Apothecary's shop with two of his friends. He had laid out a little plan to them - a little innocent mischief, as he called it.

Tanaka waited for an answer to his query. The plan sounded harmless enough, but if they got caught, the consequences did not appeal to him.

"Who will pay the money?" his cohort added.

Yamaguchi was a swarthy complexioned, slender man with a goatee and long dark hair. Tanaka was heavier set, with stubble on his chin. The pair looked sinister and threatening. Tanaka had killed a *Samurai* warrior with his own sword. Cut him in half at the waist with a two-handed swing of the victim's super sharp blade. That legend followed him wherever he went.

"It's this way," Matsui-san went on to explain again. To Yamaguchi, he said, "you climb the ladder to the room where the lad is sleeping. Very quietly. You wrap him up in a blanket and cover his mouth with what I give you, but not too tightly. Then go down the ladder and into the wagon. He will not awake. Tanaka will hold the ladder. I will drive the wagon. We take him to the abandoned farm of Akadamo's and you two keep watch over him there. I will write the ransom note and deliver it to the constable, saying I found it attached to the door of the pension. After a suitable agony for the town, I will pay the ransom - which is your wages. You give back one third to me, and Hana-ko will be in my debt eternally. Clear?"

"Suppose someone sees us?" Tanaka asked, in need of more convincing.

"In the middle of the night, no one will be moving about," answered Matsui-san.

"What about the constable on his rounds?" Yamaguchi pursued.

"Not at the time we plan," Matsui-san responded. "And we'll do it quickly. You need some practice so you can carry this out in no more than a few minutes. Are you saying you can't do it?"

"No. We can do it," answered Tanaka. "But we want a down payment on the reward, first. And we don't want to be stuck on that farm forever. That would drive me crazy. The child might drive me crazy anyway. I don't want this taking long. What if this *Koku-jin* does not leave by then?"

"That's a risk," he replied, "but one I am willing to take. If he doesn't go, I can have the cook mix some "medicine" in his soup, and he'll be ready to go soon enough."

The duo laughed coarsely, but they knew Matsui-san was serious, and he could do as he said.

"What if we are caught?" Yamaguchi intoned. "What then?"

"If you are threatened, get rid of the child and move fast. Bind him tightly and make sure he cannot yell," he replied. Then he said slowly and quietly, "do what you must do. But by all means get away as fast as you can. You are not known in this town. The post will carry any information you care to tell me. Just make sure it is disguised."

"You mean ... kill the child, if we have to?"

"No. I don't want that. But you cannot waste time being too considerate of him. There can be nothing known about this, or who was behind it. Clear?" The muscles on Matsui-san's jaw tightened at the thought of things going wrong. "We cannot have this fail," he said firmly. "I will be the savior, understand? I do not want anything to happen, except that which we plan."

A few nights later, the wagon moved quietly and slowly up to the inn. Muffled wheels and men with muffled shoes gave no sound on the cobblestone street. A wispy fog acted to conceal their movements somewhat. The cloth-wrapped ladder went in place against the wall on the side of the pension, and Yamaguchi slowly started to climb it.

But a light in the distance set the men to whispering furiously in quiet desperation.

"Walking lantern. The constable," hissed Matsui-san. "Get the ladder into the wagon. Move into the back alley and into the brewer's yard."

The ladder went back into the wagon carefully. Yamaguchi departed down the alley to open the fence gate to the yard, as Tanaka steadied the ladder in the back of the wagon.

Matsui-san's heart was pounding and his hands sweating as he eased the wagon down the alley and into the yard. Yamaguchi closed the gate.

The light passed by, as the constable made his round in the middle of the night. Thankfully he did not hear the heavily beating hearts of the conspirators, nor did he suspect.

After he had passed, they waited for a short time then opened the gate gently, and the wagon and its occupants moved silently to the back of Matsui-san's shop a few blocks away. They edged down a back alley and into a barn behind the shop. After the wagon and the horse were taken care of, the threesome engaged in a heated conversation in the dark of Matsui-san's abode.

"That was too close," exclaimed Tanaka. "What would we have said, if we had been caught?" He removed the cloth wrappings about his shoes.

"Don't worry about that," answered Matsui-san, engaged in the same undressing. "Nothing happened, and we're safe."

"But so is the child," intoned Yamaguchi.

"We will have to wait and look for our next chance," he said. "Ryoko will be near me at all times. Watch out for her. The message will come through her. Wait out of sight at Akadamo's barn. Nobody goes there. You should be safe."

"I don't like staying so close," muttered Yamaguchi. "What about Sendai ... or Yamashiro? Why couldn't we just go there and hire out as laborers. Come get us when you need us. Eh?"

"Those towns are only an hour away by carriage or horse. Ryoko could make that trip without too much trouble, no?" Tanaka was agreeing with his companion. "We'd have more freedom and no problems."

"Where would you stay?" Matsui-san asked.

"We'll find a place - a room or something." Yamaguchi assured him. "And we'll let you know where we are right away."

"Well, that might work," Matsui-san said. "I will give you part of the start-up money now. But let's decide exactly where first."

"No. Not practical," added Tanaka. "We don't know what will greet us. We need to nose around some, find work, then we'll let you know. Take maybe a few days."

"Not much else we can do now," added Yamaguchi. "I'm going to sleep."

CHAPTER 15

PRACTICE

Two nights later, the church was abuzz. The choir was all up front milling about with sheet music. Every fifth person had a copy. They could not make copies by hand for them all on such short notice. Hana-ko, along with a few other townspeople and Hanzu, were seated in the pews observing the goings on. A stirring of admiration welled up in Hana-ko's heart, as she watched Sebastian signal the choir from the console.

He pressed the keys for a scale and led them as a warm-up. Ah ah ah ah ah ... the choir responded. Up and down, a different scale now. Then the soloists - tenor, bass, and alto in turn.

He signaled again from the console. They quieted.

"All right," he announced. "We are ready. From first page please, on three." He signaled; then started to play softly on the organ from the selection *Sleepers Awake*.

The choir began and sang well under Sebastian's direction.

Hana-ko, with Hanzu beside her, closed her eyes as a good mix of voices wafted over her. The piece had a nice sonority, a kind of subtle rhythm that carried it along at a pace not too slow, not too fast. The part-singing was noticeably intriguing.

"Wow. That is really something," whispered Hanzu quietly. "Could you sing like that, Mother?"

She smiled. Yes, at one time it had been no effort, and she loved it. But that was in the past. Now she was content to be just a listener. She felt no energy to do it anymore. She watched without a twinge of jealousy or envy. They were fine. She could do better, but today was not for her.

Sebastian made a signal with his arm to indicate the end of piece.

"Very good, choir," he said, "quite good. Take the other piece home and study it for Wednesday. You are dismissed."

The choir milled about, standing down, and slowly dispersing, talking among themselves.

Hana-ko said nothing, but in a quiet way she had been moved by the music, so pensive. His music had a depth to it - a peaceful quality, something restful and magnificent at the same time. A serene confidence, something Godlike about it. She couldn't quite put her finger on it, but it did leave her with feelings.

"Principals next," Sebastian announced. "Closed audition please."

That was the signal for all to leave except those trying out for solo parts. The soloists stood, as the rest of the people, including Hanzu and Hana-ko, milled slowly out of the church.

There was no soprano.

"No soprano?" Sebastian queried in disbelief. "Is there no one here to sing solo soprano? There's always a soprano!" He was at a loss for words. "I can believe no tenor, but no soprano? Never."

Hana-ko paused for just a moment in the doorway. She sighed. No. This was not for her. Not this time.

"Ahhh, well ....," said Bach resignedly. "Let's get on with it. Bass part."

Without looking back, she left the church.

Later, after the rehearsal, Sebastian entered the inn, where Hanzu and Hana-ko sat quietly talking at the table by the window. They each had a cake and a mug of green tea for dessert, now almost finished. As he entered, the serving girl pulled a chair and placed a cake and a mug of tea for him, too. He sat down, a little tired and discouraged.

"Thank you," he said, nodding to the girl.

"You don't look very happy," offered Hana-ko quietly. "Didn't the rehearsal go well?"

The choir was good. Very decent," he responded. "They will do fine - but no soprano - no soprano at all. Isn't there anyone in this town that is willing to sing solo soprano?" He looked at Hana-ko, imploring, but firm rather than emotional. "Do you know anyone else who can help us?"

Hana-ko and Hanzu looked at each other briefly.

"Auntie Mariko," Hanzu piped up before she could answer,

"And who is Auntie Mariko?" He looked at the boy quizzically. "Is she good?"

"As good as my mother," Hanzu blurted out. Then he shot a furtive look over to Hana-ko.

She glanced back with arched eyebrows.

"Uh ... almost, almost, uh, not quite, but still good," stammered Hanzu, trying valiantly to save an awkward moment, but not entirely succeeding. "They sang all the time," he murmured.

She gave Hanzu a scolding look.

He ducked down and resumed eating his cakes.

"She is my sister," explained Hana-ko. "She lives in the next village."

"How far?" Sebastian asked, his interest starting to pick up.

"About an hour, by foot," she replied, "maybe twenty minutes by horse."

"We must fetch her tomorrow morning," he said emphatically. "We cannot go on without a soprano." Then his eyebrows raised, and he shot a sly glance at Hanzu.

Hanzu wore a questioning look at first, but then he began to get the idea. He grinned, looking knowingly at Sebastian.

"Is something going on? Did I just miss something?" Hana-ko looked back and forth between them, a little put out.

Hanzu rose from the table, almost too eagerly. "I'd better get some sleep, if I'm *riding* tomorrow." The grin was broad now, and his eyes sparkled at the adventure. "Night, mother," he said, as he leaned over and kissed her with a gentle hug. Then he turned and went up the stairs. It seemed like his feet never touched the ground.

Sebastian and Hana-ko remained at the table. He looked at her quietly in a wistful sort of way. She was beautiful. It seemed a shame that she was locked in time, unable to get beyond the past.

"Hana-ko, I told you," he began, "that I have twelve children, but in fact the count is nineteen - not all of them are alive. We have lost seven - mostly babies, but some lived long enough to be children. Very sad and painful, it took the life out of us - that a child, so innocent, should die. I, too, have felt like blaming God. It seemed so unjust. And it hurt."

"I'm sorry," she responded, pensively. "I didn't know." She lowered her head. No doubt, the thought of losing Hanzu on top of the loss of her husband was too overwhelming to think about. "Do you really understand?" She said defensively.

"It would be hard for me to really understand what is your experience uniquely. But I have lost a spouse, too. Death is no stranger. I know how I felt. I cannot know how you feel - unless you tell me. So much depends on how we take it."

"It is not a matter, always, of what we *think* about something, is it?" She challenged him.

"Life can be very hard sometimes," he responded carefully. "For a time we may have to bear sorrow. But time does not stand still; neither does God."

"That may be true," she said, a slight tinge of bitterness in her voice. "I have a very hard time feeling love for God right now. I am a woman. I have little support, except for the sewing jobs I am able to do here and there. I have Hanzu to care for. We have a little money from the sale of Takash's farm but no prospects for the future - except for men I am not interested in."

"But you have friends. Kind friends," he said.

"I am thankful, but it is not enough," she said, giving him a sharp look. "Takash was a good man, and now he is gone. And he is not coming back - ever." She was tearing up, but anger reflected in the tears.

"Hana-ko," he said quietly.

"I had a nice life," she went on, "a good life, and I was happy." A little sob escaped her lips in spite of herself. "But not now. Can't you understand?" She looked at him with that strange mixture of plaintiveness and anger he had come to expect from her. "It's not in me to do it anymore." She anticipated his direction.

"But you are trained," he continued. "You were excellent. That is something one never forgets - never loses. You cannot bury your talents. That is not the way."

She sighed. "I hear you," she said. "But it has to come from within." Her voice cracked a little bit. "It is just not there." Then her assertiveness manifested itself again. "I won't do it."

"Maybe that's the problem." He leaned back in his chair. "You won't," he mused aloud. "That can change."

"I don't think so," she said coldly. "It's a matter of the heart. I don't feel it. It's just not there. If I tried, I would only be going through the motions - like a marionette."

"Are you trying to take revenge for what happened?"

"No," she said defiantly.

He sighed again. "Ah, we are different, you and I. Perhaps a woman sees this differently than a man. For me, well ... maybe it was my profession - what people expected of me. In spite of what I felt, I still had to do my job. You can never forget the passing of your spouse - or of your child."

They exchanged looks, and she softened a bit. He was speaking from experience after all. He had been through this, too. Even though he was a man, perhaps he could have some idea what it felt like for her.

"I hope the time will come for you," he said quietly, gently, " ... when ... you can be your best self again. Maybe that is all that you need ... just time."

"Maybe."

She took a deep breath and exhaled. "I don't know how much time it will take. Will it be forever? A few more years? A few days? I just don't know."

She looked him in the eye briefly, then away.

"I'll see you tomorrow," she said softly.

Then she rose quietly, gave him a brief, plaintive look and turned and went up the stairs.

He could only hope tomorrow would bring better news.

CHAPTER 16

THE MORNING RIDE

It was about nine o'clock in the morning when Hanzu appeared riding Uesugo's horse, The horse had an unpronounceable name, but Sebastian had christened him *Braunschweiger,* because his body looked a bit like a sausage. Hanzu was all smiles and raring to go. Auntie Mariko would return in a carriage, but he had the horse all to himself for the morning and part of the afternoon. He could go by old Itahara's farm, then up by the river, then across to Nakamura's, then to Ikeda's, then to Iwakura's where he could get some great *akami* for lunch. This could be an exciting day.

"Be careful, Hanzu," implored Hana-ko, with that tone of all mothers cautioning their enthusiastic offspring. "Just go to Auntie Mariko's directly and come straight back. No wandering around. You never know who is out on the road."

"Of course, Mother," Hanzu said reassuringly, but he had other plans ... and freedom. "I will be back right after lunch."

"Mariko will come by coach," Hana-ko assured Bach, who was standing beside her.

"The horse is fine?" Bach queried.

"Yes," said Uesugo. "Hanzu knows him very well. He may not be the fastest horse in town, but he is solid, and quite comfortable with Hanzu. He will be fine."

Matsui-san stood at the back of the crowd, saying nothing. Something about the way he moved made Hana-ko uncomfortable.

"Bye, Mother," Hanzu shouted. "I'm off. Come on, *Brauni,*" he yelled to the horse, using Sebastian's nickname for the animal. He grinned and waved to them all as he turned the horse around, and with a slight kick, got him into a canter.

"I do hope he'll be all right," murmured Hana-ko with a worried frown. "Sometimes he is just too much to control."

"He'll be fine," said Uesugo reassuringly.

Hanzu was exhilarated as he made his way out of town on the road to the north. Adventure - that's what boys were made for. It was a beautiful day, sun shining brightly and puffy clouds being blown gently along by the wind. A great day, and he was not going to miss it.

Not more than ten kilometers out of town, he spied a couple of men with their horses by the side of the road. One of them motioned to him as he approached.

"Say, can you help us to get this shoe back on?" The stranger said, indicating the dappled horse at his side.

"Sure," Hanzu said, pulling up old *Brauni* and jumping off the saddle. The men looked like local farmers.

That was the last thing he remembered as he woke up on a bed in unfamiliar surroundings. His head hurt, and he was tied to the bed.

"Mama? Mama? Where are you?" He cried instinctively, and now fearful.

One of the men, swarthy with a goatee, poked his head in the door, in a little bit of bad temper. "Shut up, you idiot! The quieter you are the better it will go with you."

"Where am I?" he asked frightened and insistent. "Where's my mama?"

"Your mother's fine in town," the man replied roughly. "She'll be even finer when you get back - if you get back. And so will we - certainly richer, and that means finer, no?" He looked back into the other room at his cohort and laughed coarsely. "I'd love to be there when that *Burgomeister* gets the little letter we sent him. Ha. The look on his face would be worth half the money we'll be getting for this."

"You shouldn't tell too much," the other man added from the next room. "The little brat will think we want him to live. Good thing we got the horses when those idiots left for town, eh?"

Now Hanzu's heart was beating much faster than he had ever experienced before. "What are you going to do with me?" he asked anxiously.

"You're going nowhere," goatee man sneered. "We are going to sit here until you're rescued - by a bag of money. Simple, isn't it? If you're not quiet, or if the money doesn't show soon, then ..." He reached for a knife he held in his belt and motioned menacingly. "We'll leave you here and move on."

He caught sight of the knife and realized he could be in big trouble. And this was for real. At that moment, a horse neighed outside, and he caught a glimpse of it through the window. His head turned to follow it moving around in the yard. He was starting to think fast.

"I need the chamber pot," he said abruptly. It wasn't entirely a ruse.

"Oh, damn," said goatee man. "You go get it," he said to his cohort. "I'll watch the kid, here."

"Nothing doing," came the reply from the other man. "He's not going anywhere. You get it. I'm going to cut this fish for breakfast."

"Dammit." Goatee man partially untied him from the bed, so he could take care of his duty, looking him right in the eye. "Don't move from here," his captor said menacingly as he went back out the door, grumbling.

As soon as he disappeared from sight, Hanzu pulled at the bond around his one leg and slipped it off. Sweating, he carefully moved the other rope from his arm. They were not good knot tiers. Quickly, he moved to the window, opened it wider and bounded out. He was running for the horse when his captor returned.

Moving quickly into the yard, he found a convenient bale of hay to use as a stool. He grabbed the reins, jumped up and mounted the horse bareback. He pulled him around by the reins and galloped away, jumping the fence and heading for the woods beyond.

He stopped the horse just inside the woods, looking back to see if he was being followed.

Just then the two men burst from the house and hurriedly mounted their horses for the chase. He gave his horse a kick to urge him on, emerging out of the woods and galloping up the road to the right. The men caught sight of him and pursued quickly. He rode into the woods again, dismounted from the horse and sent it away to try to give the kidnapers the slip. He quickly climbed a tree, but the horse did not go far. The men soon overtook it.

"He's in the woods," said the heavier set man breathlessly. "Come on. But be careful. Go around the outside of the trees over there," he ordered goatee man, gesturing with his hand. "Slow. He can't outrun us."

His cohort did as he was told, and they both moved on into the woods from different angles, mounted on their horses. When they reached the clearing where Hanzu was hiding in a tree on the far side, he held his breath, praying they did not see him.

At the inn people were milling about in the street in front. Sebastian and Uesugo were in conversation. Uesugo was holding the bridle to *Brauni*. The horse had returned without its rider.

"What do you think happened?" he asked.

"I don't know," Uesugo replied. "It doesn't look good. Something must have happened. *Brauni* would not come back without Hanzu unless something happened."

A constable came out of the inn, followed by Hana-ko.

"But what happened? What could have happened to my child?" She queried insistently, though the constable could not possibly answer.

"All we know is that the horse returned without him. We will send men along the way to find out."

"Has he been kidnapped? Or has he been hurt? Why him? What will I do without my boy? My dearest love on earth?" Hana-ko was distraught. Her eyes reflected her panic. The grim faces of the crowd only made it worse.

"We need search parties immediately," the constable declared. "Everyone, anyone who wants to help is welcome! They cannot be far away, and since there is no major river near, they must have gone by horseback or wagon. Does anyone have some good dogs? We'll try to track them. It's possible also that he might be hurt. Matsui-san, we will need you."

Matsui-san was in the crowd. He nodded, but Sebastian could swear he saw the man smile ever so slightly.

"I found this on the inn door this morning," Matsui-san said with serious mien, as he handed over a piece of paper to the constable. "Kidnapers."

"Do you think kidnapers? Oh my God. Oh Hanzu," cried Hana-ko.

"Don't worry, Hana-ko." Sebastian said gently but firmly. "We will do all in our power to find him. All of us."

"This is a ransom note," said the constable, taking the paper from Matsui-san's hand. "Uh huh. It might be those horse thieves or maybe someone else. I don't know why they would do this to poor Hanzu. It seems they are holding the whole town ransom. They cannot have gotten far, so I think we need to move fast." Looking around at crowd he repeated, "Come, time's wasting. Who will help? Let's go."

There were general cries of agreement from the crowd as they dispersed into groups for the chase.

Hanzu was starting to sweat and breathe heavily as the men got closer. They were on horseback and looking down. Goatee man passed right underneath him, then went back to the clearing to meet his cohort. Suddenly, he heard familiar grunting from below and behind him. It was a wild boar nosing about in the grass and coming towards the tree he was in. An idea slowly dawned on him. At the right moment he dropped on the boar. There was terrific squealing and grunting. The boar bolted directly toward the men and their horses, guided by Hanzu's shove. The horses reared in surprise as the boar charged right into them. Both riders were thrown. Goatee man hit his head on a rock and was knocked out; the other staggered around, dazed after he picked himself off the ground.

The horses had bolted, but had not moved far, and the boar had disappeared into the woods. Trying not to show himself too much, Hanzu ran out, mounted one of the horses, grabbed the reins of the other and took off at a gallop. The man started to give chase, limping and rubbing his head, but then gave up and returned to his friend.

Hanzu rode away with the other horse in tow.

About fifteen minutes later, when he thought they were far enough away he dismounted and loosely tied the spare horse to a tree along the road. Then he mounted back up and went towards the farm of Auntie Mariko.

It took about an hour to find his way to familiar roads. Mariko was surprised to see him, as he rode up to her farm.

"Certainly I will come," she said, "but not until tonight. I have to stay here until then. You tell them, all right? But first, some water for your horse, and some food for you, no?"

"Of course," he smiled. "Thank you so," he replied. He liked Auntie Mariko. She bore only a slight resemblance to his mother. Mariko was dark haired and a little plumper. But she had an unfailingly gracious manner, and he always felt good around her. She had no children of her own, and she always made a big fuss over him. She hugged him tightly and led him inside. He said nothing about the kidnapping, so as not to alarm her. She would come by coach, anyway, and have at least the protection of the driver and footman.

The brief repast was tasty and refreshing. He would have to skip the akami at the Iwakura's. His job was done, and now he needed to get back home. No dawdling. He mounted the saddle of his captive horse and cantered away. The ride back to town could hardly be so exciting.

Not ten kilometers from Auntie Mariko's, he caught sight of a pair of men walking in front of him, trailed by a horse, which one of them held by the reins. He knew it was them. His heart beat suddenly faster, and a lump appeared painfully in his throat. His chest tightened. Fast. He had to move fast. Kicking the horse gently in the ribs he got more speed and passed them quickly. One of them cried out, and the other mounted his horse and gave chase again. Hanzu looked back anxiously. Goatee man was closing in on him, and the look on the kidnaper's face was not to be misinterpreted.

There was a side road up ahead that led to a short cut to the back end of town. He decided to take it. He pulled on the reins, but the horse wouldn't respond. He jerked on the reins to get him to turn. The horse stopped suddenly, and he felt himself coming out of the saddle and over the horse's head. He landed in the trees with a thud, and all went black.

Hanzu remembered nothing. He did not hear the kidnapers return and laugh at his plight. He did not hear the townspeople calling, nor did he hear the constable's yell when he caught sight of the kidnapers with Hanzu stretched across the saddle, the two miscreants on foot beside him, one on either side. At the yell, the kidnapers dropped Hanzu to the ground and made off on the horse, both of them in the saddle. Was there a hawk circling high above?

When the constable got to Hanzu, it was evident that he had been hurt. There was a gash on his head that was bleeding generously, and his body was limp.

"Call for a cart!" the constable said to the others. "And bring him to Matsui-san's. It looks like he is hurt bad. Tell his mother we have found him, but nothing else. You and you," he said, indicating two of the helpers, Await here with me in case those brigands return." They bent over Hanzu's body and lifted his head a little. The constable gently maneuvered his rolled up coat under the boy's head to give it support. He then poured a little water on it to clean the wound and to see how bad it might be.

"Hmmmm, it's a gash all right. A little deep. This is a job for Matsui-san," he said. Then he took a little water and moistened Hanzu's lips. They did not have long to wait.

Scores of people came out to greet them with the cart. Matsui-san was among them.

He bent down over the boy as the others stood around. "Give him some room," he said firmly, his face showing deep concern and his hands trembling a bit. The gash was sizeable. "This will need stitching. We have to get him back quickly - but carefully." Under his breath he cursed the foul-up of his plans. This was a pickle. With shaking fingers he doused some sulfur powder on the wound to keep it clean, and some astringent to slow the bleeding. Then he bandaged the boy's head. He worked carefully, quickly, but not too hurried. "No mistakes around the head," he murmured. "Careful and slow. Swelling of the brain could kill the boy." He would deeply regret that for eternity. Sweat appeared on his forehead.

"Water," he cried. "Does anyone have water?"

A few responded.

He soaked some cloths and placed them around the boy's head to keep it cool. "Not too much, not too little. Keep your fingers crossed and let's get him back to town."

He hoped to God that Yamaguchi and Tanaka would keep out of sight and never set foot in the town again. He would have to pay them to keep them quiet. If Hanzu died, they would surely sing, if caught. He could not afford that. He sweated at the thought. He would have to leave town, too - as fast as possible - but not before Hanzu was healed, and if … if.

Hana-ko's face was contorted in agony as she caught sight of Hanzu being carried into Matsui-san's back room - the emergency room. He was laid on a couch, his head carefully propped up with a soft pillow replacing the constable's coat. Matsui-san gently placed a blanket over him from feet to neck.

"This will be hard," he said to no one in particular. "We have to wake him. He will feel pain."

"Oh, no." Hana-ko gasped. "Why?"

"We cannot let him go into coma," said Matsui-san. "He could die. But let me try to stitch first." He went for the needle and thread, and carefully went about the operation as Hana-ko, shaken and wan, observed with anxious concern.

A few agonized minutes passed, then more. Matsui-san was sweating with careful effort.

"Five stitches," he said. "Done. Here." He motioned to Bach, who had just entered the shop. *"Koku-jin.* Help me with the bandages."

Bach moved over gingerly. "This is not my profession," he said hesitantly, then he added with a sigh, "but over the years, life has brought so much of this that I have become used to it."

Matsui-san placed more powders on the wound, after removing all the former bandages, and then started wrapping new ones.

Bach held Hanzu's head in his hands.

"Try not to move the head at all," he said to Bach, as he wound the cloth around Hanzu's head. "Good. That should do it. Now I have to wake him."

He went to a closet and removed a bottle. "Ammonia salt," he said matter of factly. He opened the cork and passed the opening under Hanzu's nose a few times. At first, there was no reaction.

"Ughhh," Hanzu groaned and inhaled sharply.

"Oh, Hanzu." Hana-ko exclaimed. "Hanzu." She flew to his side.

"No. Not now," said Matsui-san authoritatively. "Do not disturb him. This will take a few days. Someone must be here at all times. And for today - not you. You must go home and rest - and thank God he is back. Let us hope he makes it all the way." He had never uttered a more fervent prayer in all his life. He grabbed Hana-ko and moved her firmly away.

She resisted.

"We must listen to the apothecary," Bach said gently, as he assisted Matsui-san in moving a struggling Hana-ko into the anteroom. "He needs air and quiet," he said slowly.

"We will have Madam Yamada come," Matsui-san said. "I know she is very good at this kind of thing. The first day is very critical," he was speaking to Hana-ko softly. "After that you may come back."

"Let's go back to the inn," Bach said, taking her by the arm.

"All right," she said bravely. Her tears had not abated much, but she saw the wisdom of Matsui-san's advice. "Let's go."

Uesugo arrived as Hana-ko and Bach were leaving. "How is he?" he asked. The pair indicated Matsui-san and moved slowly by. He walked in and greeted the apothecary.

"And?" he asked.

Matsui-san waited a few moments until Bach and Hana-ko were out of hearing. "If his brain swells, he will die."

"I should not have let him go alone." Uesugo's breath came in sharply, remonstrating himself.

"We could not foresee what happened, could we?" Matsui-san was painfully aware of another, more personal, meaning to what he had just uttered. "An accident. No one is to blame."

"Do you need someone to stay?" Uesugo asked.

"Yes, thank you," he replied. "I will be gone a few hours. Madam Yamada will be here in an hour or so. Please remain until I get back. Then you may go. I will be here all night. That is the critical time."

Uesugo nodded, as Matsui-san made ready to leave. As he strode out the door, Uesugo looked back at the still form on the table. Thoughts went through his head. He was in some way responsible for this. He regretted letting Hanzu go alone with *Brauni*. He should have accompanied the boy. But the work on the organ was pressing him, and he simply assumed ... nothing would happen. He shook his head. Matsui-san would use this turn of events to his advantage. He would look like the savior. He was the essential actor on the stage - everybody else was at his beck and call. But he himself could not let Hanzu down - or Hana-ko. Whatever he could do to help, he should, and he should do it well. The results had to be left to God.

Back at the inn, Hana-ko was inconsolable.

"But Matsui-san knows what he is doing," Sebastian said reassuringly. "And there is no one else in town to do it. We must trust God."

"But he is my boy," she cried. "I should be there with him. He needs me."

"He does," he responded, "but not right now. Wait."

"I can't," she sobbed. "I *must go*."

He took a deep breath. "Hana-ko," he said quietly, "you cannot go." He paused. "I have seen Matsui-san work. He looks like a man who knows his business well, and he seems especially careful. I think we are in the best hands possible."

She looked at him plaintively and tried to nod. But her thoughts were only of Hanzu. She did not want to agree, but there was really nothing else she could do.

CHAPTER 17

AUNTIE MARIKO

Two anxious days went by before Hana-ko was allowed in to see Hanzu.

She entered the apothecary's shop quietly and carefully, then moved quickly into the anteroom. Madam Yamada came out the back room at just that moment. She was an older, more matronly woman with graying hair and a calm, firm manner.

"How is he?" Hana-ko whispered to her.

"He is responding. That is a very good sign. He is not out of danger yet, but it looks like he will make it. Matsui-san has not slept in two days."

Hana-ko's eyes arched. Something told her *Koku-jin* had been right. She softened as Matsui-san came out of the back room to greet her.

"Hello, Hana-ko," he said quietly. "I think he is doing better. He is asleep, and I don't want you to disturb him, but you can go in and look."

"Thank you." She started to move in the direction of the room. Then she halted briefly and turned. "Matsui-san, *arigatoo.*" Her voice was almost a whisper. "Thank you for all the time and effort you have spent for Hanzu. I am deeply grateful." Tears were in her eyes as she turned to enter the room.

Matsui-san had seen them. And what of it, now? The irony of the situation squeezed him in its grip. He had succeeded, but he knew the truth, and he could never forget. No, he could not have Hana-ko now. He had succeeded only to fail. He could not stay for fear of Tanaka and Yamaguchi somehow exposing his plot. They could not be trusted. They must all move and stay away forever. Maybe a big city, in the south, like Kyoto would be a good place to go.

As Hana-ko entered, she caught sight of little Hanzu resting on the couch, much as she had seen him last; only his color looked better, and he was breathing regularly - the deep, slow breaths of quiet sleep. She got a good feeling as she watched. It was a feeling of hope. She felt he was in good care. The best they had. There was nothing more to ask. Just watch and pray. A few more days, Matsui-san had said. Then maybe he would be well enough to talk. She would smother him in kisses, hold him and hug him. Oh, that voice. It was always such a boisterous thing. How many times had she scolded him? And now, she would give anything to hear it again.

Tears rolled down her cheeks, as she gazed on his face. The skin had swollen, and his head was distorted a bit, but Matsui-san had said the brain was all right. No swelling. And the wound was healing. She pitied him so. He must be feeling pain, real pain. The kind grown ups know all too well in this world. She winced at the thought of her little boy going through that ordeal. She thought about the day she would lose him. To the army, or to some trade, a journeyman making his way in life outside of their little town. That time will come. But now it could wait. She wanted her beloved boy back again.

"How is he?" A quiet voice whispered lowly. It was Sebastian.

"Oh, *Koku-jin*. He is quiet and doing well, they say," she answered. "He looks better, and yet worse."

"The wound has swollen the skin a bit," he remarked. "That is normal. It is a good sign. I hope he is not in too much pain. It is a terrible thing to see young children suffer."

"Matsui-san hasn't said. I did not ask."

"He is doing a fine job."

Hana-ko's head fell slowly. "I will come back this evening," she said and rose to leave.

As they left the room, they were greeted by Matsui-san and Madam Yamada.

"Thank you," she said quietly. "I will be back tonight. It was good to see him." She exited quickly.

However, Bach stayed behind.

"Ahh, Matsui-san," Bach began with a slight bow, "you are doing a fine job. Hanzu is dear to many, as you know."

Matsui-san nodded, giving him a cautious and quizzical look.

"He is like one of my own," said Bach affectionately as he departed. "Let us hope it all turns out well."

Matsui-san responded with the slightest bow, but he did not add to the conversation. He gave a little nervous twitch and turned to the medicines on the shelf behind him, searching through a few jars.

Bach wondered why Matsui-san was acting so odd.

"Well let us all hope the boy recovers completely," Bach added, then turned and walked out.

Rehearsals had to go on, regardless, and Sebastian did not have time to dawdle. At the console that evening, Auntie Mariko sang without Hana-ko being there. He noted that she was indeed a good singer, as she went through scales, the ah's had a sonorous quality that he liked. Then he handed her some sheet music - the *Christe* from the *Mass in B minor*, the soprano II part.

"Can you sing it?" he asked.

"I think so," she replied, glancing over the music. "Some of the high notes may be hard."

Bach started playing. She did well, and he was pleased. "Excellent," he exclaimed. "You will do well." He hesitated. "Can you sing this?" He added, handing over the soprano I part.

"I can try," said Mariko gamely, "but I am not a first soprano. The high notes ... I really have to strain to reach them. I am not my sister." She looked over the music with practiced eye, glancing here and there. The sound of footsteps on stone distracted her momentarily.

"Hello, Mariko." Hana-ko walked up the aisle of the church.

They both greeted her in return. Something seemed different in her voice, though. Some cloud had blown away. It was more that just joy at seeing her sister again.

"Your sister is here," Bach whispered to Mariko. "Do you think ...?"

"I don't know," she responded quietly.

"Excellent job, Mariko," he said loudly. "A little more work on the high notes and we'll have it. Now I need to leave for a little bit, and when I come back, we'll try again." He got up, handed Mariko some sheet music, and left.

Mariko gathered the music together, as her sister came up to congratulate her.

"Well, it seems you were very good, as usual," Hana-ko said smiling.

"Oh, you are always so kind," she responded, "but I need a little help here. Could you?" Mariko showed her the music sheets. "This is hard to reach for me," she said, indicating a particular passage. "I could never hit that well, you know. You were always so much better. How about some advice? Can I fake it with my voice if I get in trouble?" She looked at Hana-ko quizzically. "If I drop an octave, that is too much I fear. What would be better - a drop to the fifth, or the sixth?" She sighed. "I may not even be able to reach a third down. Why don't we try. You coach me, all right?"

Hana-ko nodded.

They hummed to find the key, then started. They sang, *a capella*, in unison until the high note. Then Mariko cracked it.

"Oh, there I go again," she laughed.

Hana-ko smiled an encouraging, affectionate smile.

"Let's try again," she said.

They tried a few more times to work out a suitable harmony for what Mariko could not reach. Then Bach entered through the door and approached the two.

"Oh, he's coming back," Mariko whispered, then said more loudly. "Here, why don't you do first soprano with me now? Let's try it together."

"Well? Are we ready?"

Mariko looked at her sister, Sebastian looking at them both, first one then the other.

"You go on, Mariko." Hana-ko took a deep breath and looked away. "You are doing fine. I ... cannot," she said quietly. "I can think of nothing with Hanzu in the condition he is." She looked plaintively at her sister. "I really need to be going. I cannot leave him alone for long." She turned away and walked resolutely out of the church.

Sebastian was disappointed, then a bit angry, but he held it in.

"I can sing soprano II. Can we do it with just that?" Mariko offered.

"I suppose we'll have to," he replied. He went resignedly to the console as Mariko continued to practice.

Hanzu had been moved to his room in the inn. It was here that Hana-ko was headed. She took the long way back just to walk in the cool night air and try to relax from all the tension surrounding her. The streets were quiet, and the night sky was clear. She could see well by the light of a nearly full moon. The great starry expanse seemed suddenly significant, as she gazed upward from time to time. The stars were silent, but shining, as if to speak. Their vastness was a comfort to her. But she worried minute by minute about her son's condition. Infection could set in. His wounds had to be kept clean. She could not let him sleep too long, but she hated to wake him when he would feel pain. The ammonia salt Matsui-san had given her worked well, but it seemed harsh to her. She had to watch the fever, also. One had to be careful to not cool him down too much. Just a little at a time, so the body's healing process was not interfered with overmuch. It was a strain, but her attention was total and complete.

The inn loomed ahead. She entered the outside doors and climbed the stairs to their rooms. She closed and locked the door to her room and entered the adjoining room where Hanzu lay. He was sleeping. It seemed his breathing was regular. Above the bed, on the dresser, *Koku-jin* had placed the hawk of Yonezawa - to cheer Hanzu. It was there on its perch, gazing down with fierce, unblinking eyes, watching over her son. She adjusted the light of the oil lamp and looked at his face. The color had come back well. The newest bandage did not have much blood coming through it. She touched him lightly on the shoulder and shook him gently, just a little. His eyes fluttered open for a brief second. She stroked his arm firmly.

"Uhhhhh," he said, his eyes fluttering once more. "Is that you, Mother"

"Yes, dear," she answered. "Are you feeling better?"

"Yes, a little," he responded groggily. Then he said more firmly, "I'm thirsty. Do you have some water?"

"I'll get it right away." She left the room and hurried to where a pitcher of water stood on her dresser. Pouring a cup, she returned to Hanzu. "Here. Drink carefully."

He lifted his head gingerly, as she placed the cup to his lips. He took a sip, then a gulp.

"Not too much at once," she scolded him gently, removing the cup. "Take a little at a time. Matsui-san said ..."

"Oh, Mother," Hanzu insisted. "I'm thirsty - and hungry, too, Do you have any cakes and tea? My stomach is growling. Hear?"

She gave him back the cup. He took it with his hands. She looked at him carefully and placed her hands on his forehead. It was not burning anymore. The fever had gone.

He was returning to health. Tears of joy burst from her eyes and rolled down her cheeks.

"Hanzu," she exclaimed. Then she said quickly, "Wait right here." As if he could do anything else. "I'll be right back." She hurried out of the room and went downstairs, returning a few minutes later with a cup of tea and a piece of cake. He had already finished the cup of water, and his stomach growled loudly.

"Eat," she urged him. "The fever is gone. You are going to be well. Eat."

Hanzu took a draft of the tea then bit into the cake. "Ummmm, that tastes good. I feel like I haven't eaten in weeks."

"Not too much all at once, you rascal," she uttered, almost laughing for joy.

"All right, all right," he muttered. "But this does taste good." He finished the little nourishment and lay back in the bed, closing his eyes. "Oh, I am tired," he said quietly. "But thanks for the food. That tasted really good."

She smiled as she gently kissed his cheek. "Night, Hanzu," she said in a whisper.

"You are going to be well."

He sighed and closed his eyes again. "Night, Mother," he uttered and fell asleep.

She kissed him gently on the forehead, tears still wetting her cheeks, then moved into her own room. Her heart overflowed, as she dressed for bed. Once under the covers, it almost burst.

CHAPTER 18

THE VISITOR

The big day had arrived. The town never looked so inviting. Hana-ko, with Hanzu in tow, walked through streets where brightly colored banners flew from every edifice and every corner. The church had purple and white banners flying high up on the steeple. The streets had never been so crowded. Guests had come from kilometers around. There were relatives, friends, curiosity seekers. There was a feeling in the air. Excitement. Celebration. Events like this happened only too rarely in small towns like Yonezawa. There was energy among the people in the street. Not exactly laughter - this was not a fete or a party - but a kind of eager anticipation and excitement. There was the thrill of greeting seldom-seen relatives and acquaintances from distant towns - a wonderful re-connection of friendship. Cries rang out.

"I've not seen you for years."

"How are you? How have you been?"

"And the children are so grown."

"Yes, Yoshida's father died last year, very sad."

"Your arm?"

"An argument with a horse," the laconic reply.

And on it went.

People lingered on the street as others moved slowly towards the church. The rector stood at the door greeting all those who entered. He was the picture of delight. Few men enjoyed the attention of the crowd as the rector. He relished his role as the important spiritual guide of the town. And there were no rivals to worry him.

Hana-ko with the recovering Hanzu and some of the crowd entered the church. No one was in any hurry.

"I hear *Koku-jin* is playing," a voice in the crowd said. "And he is fantastic."

"Look," exclaimed another. "A full orchestra. This will be something special."

The sound of the orchestra tuning began to fill the church. First the clear, lonely, but somehow authoritative voice of the organ sounded - a clear, piercing whistle of a flute pipe. Each instrument began to find the note. A little high, then a little low, then right on - the sonority was noticeable and arresting. Then another note sounded, higher, the same thing, different instruments. This was indeed going to be something special.

Hana-ko and Hanzu took a pew seat about mid-way down the aisle. Far enough down in front where she could see *Koku-jin* at the console, but not too close to distract him. Not many people had sat down, yet. Many were still milling about, chatting with each other, as the sounds of the orchestra tuning filled in the background. They watched as a man, well dressed, elbowed his way into church through the crowd. He entered the pew area across the main aisle from them, pausing to look around, as if in a strange place.

Then he began to mutter to himself out loud, so that others noticed and heard.

"So, this is the place. Huh," he wheezed, as he removed his dark reddish-toned floppy hat. He was of medium height, a bit flamboyant, portly and out of breath. "No mean church." He turned to a parishioner. "How did you get him? Bach, I mean. In a place like this? In this … town." His emphasis on "town" sounded a bit derisive, and his look and accent betrayed him as a foreigner. He went on.

"Must have been something. Bach just doesn't come to places like this. In fact, Bach is *always* in Leipzig. He never leaves."

He turned around to some of the others moving into pews behind him.

"That's where I'm from. Now at least. I was born in Berlin, but now I live in Leipzig - a proper city. I had business in Kyoto. The coachman said Bach would be here for a musical celebration - and he fixed the organ, I understand. Ha! Is there nothing he cannot do? I can hardly believe he would appear in a place like this, but if the coachman told me the truth, I knew I could not pass it up."

A person in the crowd to the left, recognized the man as a Jew. "Sit down, *Itzahku*," he said firmly. It's about to start." *Itzahku* was what all male Jews were called, when their names were not known.

"How do you know this *Koku-jin, Itzahku*? Another responded, "He is just a journeyman musician - an organ repairman."

"Journeyman musician?" The well-dressed man was moving to take a seat, but he continued his conversation. "Ho! An organ repairman? Hah! Was Michelangelo just a stone cutter? Was Alexander just a soldier? King Solomon just a ... a businessman?"

"We never heard of him," stated another emphatically.

"How could you? He never leaves Leipzig." *Itzahku* became disdainful. "I told you that already. What you know depends on where you have been. I go to his church every week, and I am not even Christian. I am a Jew. But I am a musician, too." He paused. "I play the bass viol." He indicated a cello bowing motion. "Not too badly either," he added with evident pride.

"So what. Sit down," came a cry from forward in the pews.

"But I would give my right arm, to play like him - to write music as he does." *Itzahku* was fired with passion now, and not used to being quiet. "No, my left arm too, my head, my hands, my feet. My eyes," he indicated such with exaggerated hand motions. "Everything," he said wheezily. "Have you never heard him play?"

"Some of us have heard him." A quiet voice spoke. It was Uesugo. "Incredible."

"Hah! That hardly describes it." *Itzahku* was not to be stopped. "Not by half. In his church - even when the sermon is bad, which it is most of the time," he said unconsciously, "you still cannot leave. You dare not even go to sleep - even for a minute. If you do, you will miss something else he does. He is the greatest organist in Germany, maybe the whole world, maybe the greatest composer that ever lived, or will ever live in all of human history, ... and I should miss this day - when he is here? Never!" *Itzahku* was becoming an orator rivaling Julius Caesar.

"Oh, be quiet," another voice piped up.

Itzahku went on as if he did not hear it. "'Cut off my right hand if I forget thee, O Jerusalem!' Only a fool would pass up this opportunity - to hear Bach, right there." His hands indicated Bach bending over the console. "Right in front of you." His voice was more hushed now. "Alive, fresh, somehow a divine presence - making music like you never heard before. Every movement full of grace. Every note perfection." There were almost tears of joy in his eyes, "and you are *there*. And you know it's happening for the first time in all the world." He shook his head. "A window to heaven," he said in an almost worshipful tone. "And when he does a repeat ... ah, it is even better, if that is possible." He shook his head as if to express disbelief. Then with feeling he exclaimed, "That he is a German makes me jealous! But I say - the soul who is indifferent to this," he shrugged his shoulders expressively, looking at persons in the crowd pointedly – "deserves his own judgment."

"Sit down, *Itzahku*. You are not the rector."

"We'll see soon enough."

"Come on ... quiet. This is church, not the tavern."

The normally polite Japanese were stirred by the occasion and compelled to participate in it. The buzz in the crowd continued, as *Itzahku* took his seat - slowly, with a little effort.

Most of the people had come in and filled the pews. Matsui-san came up quietly behind Hana-ko and Hanzu. He leaned over the pew and greeted them.

"How are you, Hanzu?" he asked quietly in his most caring professional tone. Hanzu was still wearing the head bandage.

"I am much better, thanks to you, Matsui-san," replied Hanzu gratefully. "I am so happy to be here to watch *Koku-jin*," he said.

"Ahh, Matsui-san, ..." began Hana-ko. "I ..."

"Say nothing, Hana-ko. It's all right," replied Matsui-san quietly, just the slightest nervousness betraying itself. He looked anxiously at the crowd coming in, his eyes darting to and fro quickly. No ... his friends had not come.

"No, Matsui-san, I must thank you for all you have done." She hesitated just a little then turned her head quickly away. He took a spot behind them in the pews.

The plate for the offering was being passed early. They did not want to disturb the flow of the concert with an offering in the middle. Ushers moved the plates from pew row to pew row with practiced professionalism. One of them went to bypass *Itzahku*, but *Itzahku* would have none of it. He indicated with his hands to hold the plate while he searched his purse. A few seconds of puffing and wrestling with the purse and out came two gold coins - which he placed quietly and firmly in the basket. The usher looked at it a moment, completely taken by surprise, then moved on with his duty, his face betraying no further expression.

Hanzu stared at the coins in the plate before passing it on to Hana-ko, and from there, down the pew on their side.

"Mother," Hanzu whispered, "was that was a gold ducat? Two of them? I never saw such a piece of gold in my life. Why did he do that? He is not even Christian."

But Hana-ko was already thinking. Something had registered within her soul. She had heard the exchanges between *Itzahku* and the parishioners. A feeling crept over her. Was it embarrassment? Guilt? A little shame?

A little push at her obdurate and immovable attitudes? Her persistent ungratefulness? Was God questioning, challenging her? There was a struggle within. She looked up and watched *Koku-jin* a bit, and considered all that had been said. Then she exchanged glances with Hanzu.

Perhaps this was the time. And it would not come again. The time for her to respond to all that had happened. Hanzu was back. The organ was fixed. She had been through more pain and joy in the last few weeks than ever in her life. Perhaps she should not miss this. Perhaps, it was time. After a few more pensive seconds, her face registered a decision. She rose firmly and went to the front. Hanzu fell back into the pew with a look of confusion and wonder.

Up front, she approached Sebastian at the console. Not a second later, Mariko joined them. There was talk. There was a hug from Mariko. He took out some sheet music from his bag on the floor next to the console and gave it to Hana-ko, looking at her, as if to say, "Are you sure you can do this?"

She nodded. She stayed up front, taking a seat in the first pew and looking intently through the music he had given her.

The congregation and guests had finally seated themselves, and the celebration was about to begin. Six trumpeters gathered quietly at the front near the raised platform for the choir. They stood behind the orchestra seated in chairs down on the floor, right below.

CHAPTER 19

CELEBRATION SUNDAY

As Sebastian moved around on the console bench, readying everything, Hanzu stared at his mother in complete surprise, wondering ... was she going to sing again? What changes would that bring? Sebastian signaled from the organ, and Hanzu turned his attention back to the goings on. There was a separate conductor for the orchestra. He moved into position; Sebastian signaled again, and the music started.

The trumpets sounded with the prelude to the Sinfonia from the *Easter Oratorio*. He read this from the program. The sound was authoritative, vigorous, exciting, a loud and joyous announcement of rejoicing. There was a general buzz of surprised approval from those crowded together in the pews. Trumpets and drums; this was exciting. This piece moved. The rhythms were pronounced, persistent. It made his pulse pound. And the theme was rousing. Uplifting. There was an antiphonal quality to the music, groups of instruments answering the lead trumpets, as if in conversation. The ornamentation was masterful, and the audience waited eagerly and expectantly for more.

When they finished, the trumpeters slowly took their places down among the orchestra. The choir rose - like a huge wave, all at once, but not sharply. Now, there would be singing. The bulletin handed out by the ushers proclaimed *Introit: Kyrie.*

This was the mysterious, plaintive call to God from the *Mass in B minor*, one of the most sublime, expressly Christian works in the history of music. Hanzu felt a strange awe; the congregants must have felt it, too. The passage had been edited and only lasted about a minute for the Introit. But the music could not help but rouse them - touch their hearts and engage their minds. The full choir gave voice to the text. The harmonies of the singers, the intertwining lines, the mastery of musical motion and the clarity of the voices was captivating. The haunting call *"Kyrie, Eleison"* – 'Lord, lord, ... lord have mercy' echoed in its Greek form. He gave them just the introduction, ending with the wonderful sonority for full choir, the "son" part stretched out for a full two bars.

Next, they all rose for the first hymn. They were assisted by the choir.

"Sleepers Awake," said the line in the program. Sleepers, awake. Hanzu smiled at the thought, but others may have been moved more deeply. What could it mean? Who was asleep?

The hymn ended, and the congregation and choir sat. Yoshi-ban, the monk, rose from his position on the right side of the altar and went to the lectern on the left, as the parishioners and guests saw it. It was time to open the Scripture.

Yoshi-ban opened the large Bible on the lectern and began. "The reading from the Old Testament is taken from

Psalm 25. A Psalm of David," he said in his best official voice. The not unfamiliar cries of David passed through the ears of the congregants. "Unto thee O Lord, do I lift up my soul ..." "Let not mine enemies triumph over me ... lead me in thy truth and teach me ... turn unto me and have mercy upon me."

As Yoshi-ban finished the reading, the congregants added, responsively, "Thanks be to God."

It was time for the Offertory, but no plates were being passed. Bach moved over to the orchestra to direct for the piece. Mariko rose to sing.

... And then his mother rose, too.

A murmur of surprise and approval moved through the congregants.

"O my God, it's Hana-ko," several voices exclaimed quietly.

"Oh Hana-ko. She hasn't sung for years."

"Could not sing after her husband died."

"Something must have happened."

"I wonder what? What could have happened?"

"Who cares? Don't even ask. It will be lovely to have her back."

"Something really special. I can hardly wait."

Hana-ko and Mariko readied themselves up front. Smiling they looked at *Koku-jin*, who gave the signal and the orchestra started.

The Christe from the *Mass in B minor* - a lovely duet between first and second soprano with beautifully flowing music - smooth, fluid - the rhythm carrying the music along in a subdued, but persistent pace. Hana-ko's voice rang clear and lovely, beautifully nuanced, plaintive at times, insistent at others, and Mariko sang with perfect harmony and counterpoint. The music rose and fell along with its message - *Christe, Eleison* - Christ, have mercy - the simplest of prayers. There was a personal quality to the duet, warm and close - not like the mysterious, cosmic, distant quality of the *Kyrie.* It was a lovely moment - breathtaking. As they ended the piece, many parishioners had their heads bowed and their eyes closed. It was a touching performance, a feeling of something long dead coming to life again.

As Sebastian and the two sisters sat down, the rector arose and went to the pulpit to give the reading from the New Testament and to deliver his sermon.

The rector began, warming to his task, "*Ohayo gozimasu!* Good morning! This is a wonderful morning - for us especially. I will not be long in preaching this morning. For the organ is fixed. Hallelujah! And today we are celebrating. Thank you all for responding to our invitation. It is indeed a special day. It reflects the greatest purpose of God - to restore, to redeem, to buy back, as it were, sinners from the road to hell. Just think of what Jesus did - so much healing - the man at the pool of Bethsaida - blind Bartimaeus - the demoniac, so many others. In Luke 17 we find the story of the ten lepers. Let us read and remember - for it is all too easy for us to forget and become complacent."

The rector began the reading from the New Testament. His warm and enthusiastic voice was a comfort to the parishioners.

"And it came to pass, as he went to Jerusalem, that he passed through the midst of Samaria and Galilee. And as he entered into a certain village, there met him ten men that were lepers, who stood afar off. And they lifted up their voices and said, 'Jesus, Master, have mercy on us.' And when he saw them, he said unto them, 'Go show yourselves unto the priests.' And it came to pass, that as they went, they were cleansed. And one of them, when he saw that he was healed, turned back, and with a loud voice glorified God. And fell down on his face at his feet, giving him thanks, and he was a Samaritan. And Jesus answering said, 'Were there not ten cleansed? But where are the nine?'"

He closed the Bible and addressed the congregants. "May God grant to us - always to be the one who returned - never to forget. That is the message for today. We were desolate, despondent and afflicted. That which helped us to touch the face of God in song was lost and gone, but *Koku-jin* has fixed the organ! And now we have our heart back in the church - for where is worship without music? And so today - let us continue to celebrate - with music and give God thanks."

After his brief homily, he stepped down. There was a moment of quiet. Then Hana-ko rose with Sebastian. Hana-ko alone.

More agitated whisperings swept through the congregation. The Bulletin gave the translation of the Latin *Laudamus* Te - We praise you, we thank you. Sebastian started the orchestral introduction. This was another selection from the *Mass in B minor,* and demanded a higher level of musical skill.

To Hanzu's utter delight and amazement, his mother negotiated the leaps and changes in expression beautifully and perfectly. She sang one repeat. She took a deep breath before the repeat that even he could hear, and that accentuated the specialness of the moment for them all.

Laudamus te, We praise you

benedicimus te,   we bless you,

adoramus te, we worship you,

glorificamus te.   we glorify you.

The music had a more inward quality to it. Pensive, but filled with a wonder and heart appreciation for the Creator. It was reverent and full of feeling. The musical writing and the accompaniment were utter marvels to behold.

The look on his mother's face was hard to describe. Passion? Intensity? Earnestness? Was there a trace of delight betrayed in the eyes and a union with the music and the message almost hidden in the soul?

Both Hanzu and Mariko observed intently with pounding heart. He noticed his aunt close to tears. Hana-ko was not only beautiful, but her singing was all they had heard it could be. Surpassing excellence and feeling. And there was something else - a passion, a vibrant feeling of life.

The listeners were silent as Hana-ko sat down. Then the choir rose *en masse*, and he could feel something coming. There was a slight pause. Then the finale thundered as if falling from the heavens above.

The triple *forte* of the *Sanctus* sounded suddenly with a loud noise that roused him from his seat and caught all the parishioners by surprise. A proclamation from heaven itself, so it seemed. The falling two-note theme of *Sanc-tus* coupled with the incredible intricacies of the voices, rising in tone, made it seem as if God himself was talking to man, and man was responding with worship.

> *Sanctus, Sanctus, Sanctus Dominus Deus Sabaoth.*
>
> *Pleni sunt caeli et terra gloria tua.*
>
> (Holy, Holy, Holy Lord God of hosts.
>
> Heaven and earth are full of your glory.)

As the piece went on, the four-part harmonies and sonorities, the incredible weaving of simultaneous melodies in perfect rhythm and harmony, and the sheer artistry awed Hanzu and the listeners. How could anyone write music like this?

When the choir finished, Sebastian returned to the console, and the rector went again to the lectern to give the benediction.

"Please stand," intoned the rector at his portentous best, "to receive the benediction."

The congregants stood.

"God be merciful to us," the rector quoted from Psalm 67, "and bless us, and cause his face to shine upon us. Amen. Go in peace and greet one another. The service has ended."

It was a simple benediction, nothing flowery, nothing added to the magnificence that had just gone before. Hanzu stood with the congregants stood and received the benediction. He was glad and sad at the same time, for he knew such a day would not come again in this small town.

It was a day to remember forever; a wonderful day, and he would do his best to keep the memory alive.

Sebastian began the organ postlude.

It was the *Fugue in F major* with its famous pedal point and constantly rising theme signifying insistent good cheer and generating a happy mood. It seemed like *Koku-jin* had relaxed and was actually having fun at the organ this time. The mood of the congregants broke to warm and excited conversation. Somehow they all knew what a special time this had been, and they were not going to let it go so quickly. The celebration of music was over, but the celebration of the heart was continuing. They filed out of the church slowly, in groups, still talking. The rector stood at the doors, greeting people with a warm and happy demeanor. People continued to mill about outside the church, especially congregating around Hana-ko and Hanzu.

Hana-ko received many warm congratulations, which somehow seemed to lighten her demeanor by the minute.

Hanzu was amazed by it all.

CHAPTER 20

FAREWELL

It had been a wonderful day, but Sunday could not last forever. Sebastian's job was done, and he had to be off. It was Monday, and the coach was ready. The day was clear with a few white, puffy clouds ambling slowly across a bright, medium-blue sky. The temperature was moderate, and a slight breeze blew now and then. Sebastian was standing in the street, his bags at his feet, as a small crowd gathered to wish him well. Hana-ko, Hanzu, Mariko and Uesugo stood closely by.

"Well, *Koku-jin*." The rector approached. "What is there to say? Thank you from our hearts seems so insufficient. We are so grateful. We wish you all the peace and happiness you have brought to us."

"Thank you, Rector," he responded. "All glory to God. We are just His servants."

"Ah, you are too modest," the rector intoned, "but glory to God, indeed."

Hanzu went up to him wearing a sad face. A new bandage was in place, and his head was healing now. He gave Sebastian a longing look. "Please come back," the boy said plaintively, and hugged him.

Hanzu's plea brought tears to Hana-ko's eyes. She looked at Sebastian briefly. They both knew that his request would be impossible. He had been here once. That was all they would see of him. But they would have memories. She had seen to that. She had asked him to copy out the *Laudamus* piece for her. He had done it gladly. It was done hurriedly and not completely, but enough for her to perform it in the future.

Uesugo came up to him and shook his hand warmly.

"Thank you so much for all your help, Uesugo," he said warmly. "I appreciated your skill and your friendship. God bless."

"It was the privilege I knew it would be," Uesugo responded. "I'm so glad we were able to do it."

He took Uesugo aside a bit and spoke quietly out of the earshot of the others. "I leave little Hanzu to your oversight. Hana-ko has agreed that he can apprentice in your shop. I'm sure you know what a bright lad he is, a wonderful helper and a willing worker. I am glad you are going to pay him. I know it is not customary, but it will help them both. My best wishes for your winning her. I would love to see it, but I must be off."

Uesugo stepped back into the crowd a little, and Hana-ko came up and spoke, her eyes misting over a bit, "*Laudamus te. Benedicimus te.* I will never forget you. Thank you. Thank you."

"Nor I you," he said quietly. "God bless. I am so glad Hanzu is better. I would have been inconsolable, if my little helper were not able to witness our victory. My best wishes for you. May your singing be blessed in the service of God."

She bowed her head quietly.

"I must be off." He patted her lightly on the shoulder.

"*Sayonara.*"

Rivulets of tears started flowing down Hana-ko's face, and Sebastian knew that the special Japanese meaning of the "good-bye" had registered deeply and sadly in her heart. He tried to suppress his own feelings of sadness.

As he stepped up the stairs to enter the coach, the footman moved to close the door. Once inside, he rolled down the window, as the coachman took the bags and secured them in the rear of the coach. Hanzu moved up to the window, and Sebastian stretched out his hand to touch the boy's.

"Remember, Hanzu, to be good at anything, you must practice. And whatever you become, do it with your whole heart."

Hanzu was crying softly and did not let go. His head nodded as he managed to choke out, "I learned so much from you, and I had so much fun. Won't you come back some time?"

Sebastian smiled. "In some ways, I will never leave. I will always be in your mind, and you in mine."

Their hands finally parted as the coachman called out, "Yamagata city next - about an hour." He mounted to the driving bench along with the footman. The reins for the horses were shaken, and the coach started moving away slowly.

The small group stood on the street and waved. Sebastian stuck his head out of window opening in the door and waved, continuing to watch them as the coach moved on. They were small dots in the distance, when he gave a big sigh and sat back in the seat, watching the countryside go by, once again. And then he fell asleep.

Hands were suddenly shaking him, as he groggily looked up and tried to grasp his whereabouts.

"Herr Bach!" the footman intoned. "Wake up. We are here - in Esseldingen. The boy and his mother want to ask you something."

"What? Wha? Where am I?" he muttered, rubbing his eyes. Had it all been a dream? Where was Hana-ko? Where was Hanzu? Where was the small church? The apothecary? Uesugo? Where was ... Japan?

Anna and Hans approached the open door of the coach.

"Well, Herr Bach," began Anna. "Will you stay? Will you try to fix the organ?"

Hans looked at him expectantly.

"Well, I ..." he stammered. "I, that is, ..." He moved to sit up more and knocked his satchel over, books and sheet music spilling onto the floor of the coach and out the door.

"Oh, my!" Bach exclaimed, as he looked at the scattered papers. He started immediately to pick up what he could, before the wind blew them away. The others began to help.

In the act of stuffing papers back into his briefcase, his hand encountered something rough. He pulled it out and looked at it quizzically. It was a healthy curl of wood shaving. He smiled. Probably got there from his son Carl, who had been whittling a *Blockflöte* before he left.

At that moment a small shadow rushed past them on the ground. It startled them all with its suddenness and speed.

"Look! A hawk!" the coachman exclaimed, staring upward.

"Up there," the footman added, pointing in the direction of the soaring bird.

They all stopped and looked at the magnificent, purposeful ease with which the bird circled. Its eyes appeared to be looking down unwaveringly.

"He hardly moves his wings," the coachman uttered. "Makes it look so easy. A little wiggle on the end of one wing, a dip of the other, and he circles, his eyes always on what is below. Watching intently. Looking for a meal, I think!"

But Bach's mind was elsewhere, as he observed the hawk and twiddled the wood shaving between his fingers. A wave of emotion washed over him. Then with a deep breath, he turned to his fellow travelers and spoke.

"Of course," he said with not a shade of doubt in his voice or his heart. "Of course I will come."

THE END

POSTLUDE - MUSICAL SOURCES

The reader may wish to explore the musical sources that play a role in the text. Consulting catalogs at a good music store would be a good start, but some recordings may be obscure. To that end I have listed below my main sources for the selected works. Happy listening!

MUSIC SELECTION SUMMARY LIST

1. Handel Selections

    See How the Conquering Hero /*Judas Maccabeus*

    I woo to hear thine evensong/*L'Allegro ed il Penseroso*

    Messiah

2. Sleepers Awake (Cantata 140) - Guitar

3. Prelude I - Guitar

4. Minuet in G, Anh. 116

5. Fugue in G minor "Little"

6. Dir, dir, BWV 299

7. Fugue in G, "the Jig"

8. Toccata of Toccata, Adagio & Fugue in C

9. Passacaglia of Passacaglia and Fugue in C minor

10. Fugue of T.A.&F. in C

11. Sleepers Awake - Chorus

12. Christe, Mass in B minor

13. Sinfonia, Easter Oratorio

14. Kyrie, Mass in B minor

15. Christe, Mass in B minor

16. Laudamus Te, Mass in B minor

17. Sanctus, Mass in B minor

18. Toccata in F